TEEN H P9-DMA-179

The misfits

Howe, James.

The Misfits

Other Books by
JAMES HOWE

Novels
A Night Without Stars
Addie on the Inside
Morgan's Zoo
The Watcher
Totally Joe

Edited by James Howe
The Color of Absence: Twelve Stories
 About Loss and Hope
13: Thirteen Stories That Capture the
 Agony and Ecstasy of Being Thirteen

Sebastian Barth Mysteries
What Eric Knew
Stage Fright
Eat Your Poison, Dear
Dew Drop Dead

Bunnicula Books
Bunnicula (with Deborah Howe)
Howliday Inn
The Celery Stalks at Midnight
Nighty-Nightmare
Return to Howliday Inn
Bunnicula Strikes Again!
Bunnicula Meets Edgar Allan Crow

**Tales from the House of
Bunnicula**
It Came from Beneath the Bed!
Invasion of the Mind Swappers
 from Asteroid 6!
Howie Monroe and the Doghouse
 of Doom
Screaming Mummies of the Pharaoh's
 Tomb II
Bud Barkin, Private Eye

The ~~Amazing~~ Odorous Adventures
 of Stinky Dog

Bunnicula and Friends
The Vampire Bunny
Hot Fudge
Scared Silly
Rabbit-cadabra!
The Fright Before Christmas
Creepy-Crawly Birthday

Pinky and Rex Series
Pinky and Rex
Pinky and Rex Get Married
Pinky and Rex and the Mean
 Old Witch
Pinky and Rex and the Spelling Bee
Pinky and Rex Go to Camp
Pinky and Rex and the New Baby
Pinky and Rex and the Double-Dad
 Weekend
Pinky and Rex and the Bully
Pinky and Rex and the New Neighbors
Pinky and Rex and the Perfect Pumpkin
Pinky and Rex and the School Play
Pinky and Rex and the Just-Right Pet

Picture Books
There's a Monster Under My Bed
There's a Dragon in My Sleeping Bag
Teddy Bear's Scrapbook
 (with Deborah Howe)
Horace and Morris but mostly Dolores
Horace and Morris Join the Chorus
(but what about Dolores?)
Kaddish for Grandpa in Jesus'
 name amen
Horace and Morris Say Cheese
 (which makes Dolores sneeze!)

The Misfits

JAMES HOWE

ATHENEUM   New York   London   Toronto   Sydney

ATHENEUM BOOKS FOR YOUNG READERS
An imprint of Simon & Schuster Children's Publishing Division
1230 Avenue of the Americas, New York, New York 10020
This book is a work of fiction. Any references to historical events, real people,
or real locales are used fictitiously. Other names, characters, places, and incidents
are products of the author's imagination, and any resemblance to actual events
or locales or persons, living or dead, is entirely coincidental.
ATHENEUM BOOKS FOR YOUNG READERS is a registered trademark of Simon & Schuster, Inc.
For information about special discounts for bulk purchases, please contact Simon & Schuster
Special Sales at 1-866-506-1949 or business@simonandschuster.com.
The Simon & Schuster Speakers Bureau can bring authors to your live event.
For more information or to book an event, contact the Simon & Schuster Speakers Bureau
at 1-866-248-3049 or visit our website at www.simonspeakers.com.
Also available in an Atheneum Books for Young Readers hardcover edition
Book design by Ann Bobco
The text for this book is set in Meta Book.
Manufactured in the United States of America
10 9 8 7
The Library of Congress has cataloged the hardcover edition as follows:
Howe, James, 1946–
The misfits / by James Howe.
p. cm.
Summary: Four students who do not fit in at their small-town middle school
decide to create a third party for the student council elections to represent
all the students who have ever been called names.
ISBN 978-0-689-83955-9 (hc)
[1. Schools—Fiction. 2. Elections—Fiction. 3. Friendship—Fiction. 4. Teasing—Fiction.]
1. Title.
PZ7.H8377227 Mg 2001
[Fic]—dc21 00-066390
ISBN 978-0-689-83956-6 (pbk)
0311 FFG

To Zoey

I

SO HERE I am, not a half-hour old as a tie salesman and trying to look like I know what I am doing, which have got to be two of the biggest jokes of all time, when who should walk into Awkworth & Ames Department Store but Skeezie Tookis.

Now ordinarily I would be happy to see Skeezie, do not get me wrong. In my book, he is a fine fellow, although I have heard him more than once referred to as "that young hooligan." I suspect this may have to do with his fondness for black leather jackets and slicked-back hair, combined with a certain carelessness in the area of personal hygiene and what I guess you might call a direct manner of speaking, even to those of a more advanced generation. But all I can say is that if you are willing to dig below the surface, you will discover the real Skeezie Tookis, and there you will find as big a heart as was ever produced by the little town of Paintbrush Falls, New York.

If I seem to be going on at some length to defend a character you have barely met (remember, I myself have only just glimpsed him coming toward me through Ladies' Wear & Accessories, batting at the rows of white cotton nightgowns with hands that look like they may have spent the previous twenty minutes digging a nickel out of a recently tarred road); if, as I say, I am defending him before you've even met him, it is because of the look on my boss's face as he, too, beholds Skeezie's approach.

The manager of the Men's Wear & Accessories department is a Mr. Kellerman, although I have already learned that employees under a certain age refer to him as Killer Man. Apparently, he only smiles in private, if then, and he certainly isn't smiling this particular Friday afternoon.

"It is highly irregular," he told me right off the bat when I showed up for work after school, "to hire a twelve-year-old as a tie salesman."

"Yes, sir," I said, trying to hide my light under a bushel, as my father had that morning advised me. He told me it might not pay to show off how smart I am. Well, I may be smart, but I did not get what a light and a bushel had to do with each other or anything at all, for that matter, but at the moment that was beside the point. I suspect it still is.

"Stock boy, fine," Killer Man went on, polishing his glasses with the fine silk handkerchief he'd pulled out of the breast pocket of his gray flannel blazer. It is only September and it is still hot in Paintbrush Falls, even if we are pretty far north, but Killer Man has decided, I guess, that the season dictates gray flannel.

"I worked as a stock boy over the summer," I told him.

"I am aware of that," Killer Man said.

"In the lawn furniture and garden department."

"Yes. It's on your record." He snapped his silk handkerchief in my direction, then shoved it back in his pocket with—there's no other word for it— panache. You have to hand it to the guy, he has style, even if he has the personality of a doorstop.

"Well," he said, sighing dramatically, "it seems that I am stuck with you."

"Only two afternoons a week," I pointed out. "And the occasional Saturday."

"I shall remember to count my blessings."

"Yes, sir," I said.

So Killer Man hasn't taken his eyes off me the whole half hour I've been standing here trying to look like I know what I am doing, although in point of fact I have been doing zip, when along comes, of all people, Skeezie Tookis, on whom Killer Man is now getting ready to move in, and he doesn't even know yet that the young hooligan is *my* friend. And all I'm thinking is, once he does, I'm done for. I'll be canned before I box my first tie. And I don't even want to think what my father will have to say about it.

I decide to head trouble off at the pass. I make my move.

"Excuse me, Mr. Kellerman," I say, "I think I see a customer who needs my assistance."

"If you are referring to that young hooligan," Killer Man says (you could chip ice off the words), "Security will take care of him. Don't waste your time."

4

"Oh, it's not a waste of my time, Mr. Kellerman," I say. Then, remembering something I read in the six stapled pages Awkworth & Ames gives its new employees, I add, "A customer waiting for assistance is a friend waiting to be made."

Killer Man grimaces, but there's not a whole lot he can say to that. I smile a little smugly. I suspect some of my light is leaking out from under its bushel.

"What are *you* doing here?" I hiss at Skeezie. I do not mean to be hostile, but with Killer Man hanging out behind me like a vulture in the wind, I've got to act fast.

"The question is, What are *you* doing here?" Skeezie asks back. "Geez, look at you. Tie and all."

He starts to finger my tie, but I don't let him. "It's not mine," I tell him. "If I get it dirty, I have to pay for it out of my salary."

"What kind of stinkin' rule is that?" Skeezie retorts. "Is that your boss over there? The Grim Reaper? I'm going to go right over there and tell him, What kind of stinkin' rule is that?"

I put my hand on Skeezie's chest. "Don't," I say. "Okay? I need this job. If my dad didn't used to work here, I wouldn't have this job. So do not mess it up for me, do you hear what I am telling you, Skeezie? Are you reading me, loud and clear?"

With Skeezie it is sometimes necessary to say things more than once.

"Yeah, fine," says Skeezie. "I get it. But maybe I'll write a letter to Misters Awkworth and Ames."

"You do that," I say.

"I'll bet Misters Awkworth and Ames are dead," he goes, picking at his teeth with a grotty thumbnail. "I mean, this store is like a thousand years old, man. Who shops in here anyway?"

I do not have an answer for this. In my half hour as a junior tie salesman, I have not seen another living soul, except for Killer Man, who is questionably living and arguably without a soul, and now Skeezie Tookis, who is definitely not shopping—except maybe for trouble.

We stop talking for a minute and I wonder when the Skeeze is going to get down to business and tell me the purpose of his visit. Killer Man harrumphs in the background.

"So what's up?" I say at last. "I gotta get back to work."

"Yeah, that boss of yours is burnin' holes in your shirt with his eyes. I hope it's yours, at least. Otherwise, you're going to have to pay for the damaged goods out of your salary."

"Very amusing. So," I repeat, "what's up?"

Skeezie puts a filthy hand on my shoulder and I am glad the shirt I am wearing is in fact my own. "Bobby," he says, giving me that deep look he uses to hypnotize his victims when he's about to hit them up for something. Only this time he isn't hitting me up for anything other than my attention.

"Bobby," he says again, "what day of the week is it?"

"Friday," I give back.

"And what happens on Fridays after school?"

"I go to work at Awkworth & Ames Department Store."

"As of when?"

"As of today."

"And what, may I ask, about the Forum?"

"The Forum?" I ask stupidly, because I know exactly of what he is speaking.

Skeezie squeezes his eyes tight and nods his head back and forth, like he's in pain or something. Only I know it isn't pain, because I know this look of his and what it is, is he's telling you how disappointed he is in you. Like you've done some terrible thing that has just put a dent in the perfect silver goblet that is his life.

"Bobby, Bobby, Bobby," he croons, his eyes still squeezed up as tight as if there was a whole pan of frying onions right there in front of him.

"Listen," I tell him, "I gotta go. I'm sorry about the Forum. Maybe we can do it another day."

Skeezie's eyes pop open like his head is a car that's just been rear-ended.

"Another day? Did I hear you right? What about *tradition*, my man? I got two people sittin' down the street at the Candy Kitchen, sittin' in *our* booth, Bobsters, the back booth with the torn red leatherette upholstery. They have sent me as their emissary, because we cannot begin the Forum until all are present and accounted for. And you are telling me *another day?*"

"Mr. Goodspeed," I hear behind me. It is the voice of the executioner.

8

"Really, I gotta go," I tell Skeezie.

Skeezie removes his hand from my shoulder and brushes it off on his jeans, like he'd just picked up some germs or something from my clean shirt, and says, "You can't let us down, man."

And I say, "I don't get out of work until five. Tell Addie and Joe I'm sorry. Maybe I can get my days switched here and *next* Friday—"

Skeezie walks away, shaking his head.

Killer Man harrumphs again and says behind my back, "Perhaps next Friday you will no longer be working here at all, Mr. Goodspeed."

And I think, *How come life always has to be so complicated? Will it get any easier when I'm an adult?*

And then my dad's life comes to mind and I think, *No way.*

A few minutes later, I'm watching Killer Man from out of the corner of my eye and he's standing there tapping his foot and checking his watch, waiting, I figure, for a customer to show up or another day to end, and I'm guessing his life isn't complicated at all. But

I'm also guessing that it isn't happy. What Killer Man's life mostly comes down to, I figure, is waiting.

All of a sudden, my mixed-up, preadolescent life seems pretty good. Even working as a tie salesman at Awkworth & Ames Department Store seems pretty good. Because I'm only twelve and I'm just passing through. Mr. Kellerman is stuck here for the rest of his life, with his silk color-coordinated ties and pocket handkerchiefs, waiting every day for a voice to announce, "Shoppers, the store will be closing in fifteen minutes."

And when the store does close, where does he go? My mind draws a blank.

SKEEZIE TOOKIS is not the only one who gets names slapped on him just on account of how he looks. Names come Addie's way, too, only in her case it is because of her being so tall, in addition to the factor of her intelligence, both of which fall on the plus side of the ledger if you happen to be a boy and are major liabilities if you were born into the world a girl. At least, that is my impression of how it goes in the dreaded middle-school years. I will not speak for high school, having neither firsthand experience nor an older sibling to shed wisdom on the subject.

As for Joe, well, he's been called more names than the world's most stinking umpire. He even gives himself names, although they are not bad ones and would appear to arise out of a creative urge that runs deep in him. Joe is the most creative person I know—*too* creative for some people, and maybe that is part of the problem. The other part of the problem is that he acts more like a girl than a boy much of the time, and this makes people nervous. Especially other boys. Joe figures he is who he is and what's the big deal, and I figure he is right about that.

Me, I've been called, amongst other things, Pork Chop, Roly-Poly, Dough Boy, and Fluff. I hated that last one most of all. It was the name of choice back in third grade when I ate peanut butter and Marshmallow Fluff sandwiches every day for lunch. Everybody called me Fluff that year. Or almost everybody. Not my best friends. And not the teachers. They called me Bobby or Robert, and they were all very nice to me that year, as if I had special needs. Which I guess I would have to say I did. But the way I figure it is, Who *doesn't* have special needs?

Anyway, most of the kids called me Fluff, and I kept thinking, *This is so stupid, because there's a lot more to me than half of what I put in a sandwich.* Though I expect the name had more to do with the obvious *results* of eating nonstop Marshmallow Fluff than the fact of doing it. But still, I wonder if maybe everybody gets names hung on them for only a little part of who they are.

Maybe even Killer Man.

Kids who get called the worst names oftentimes find each other. That's how it was with us. Skeezie Tookis and Addie Carle and Joe Bunch and me. We call ourselves the Gang of Five, but there are only four of us. We do it to keep people on their toes. Make 'em wonder. Or maybe we do it because we figure that there's one more kid out there who's going to need a gang to be a part of. A misfit, like us.

Sometimes I am sitting with Addie and Joe and Skeezie at lunch—at our table way off to the side and down at the end of the cafeteria, out of harm's way— and I get to thinking in a philosophical manner and what I'm thinking is this: Maybe it's the whole rest of the seventh grade at Paintbrush Falls Middle School who's misfits. Maybe when they grow up and go out into the big, wide world, they will see that Paintbrush Falls was the only place they could ever feel at home, because the rest of the world is made up of people more like me and the rest of the Gang of Five and Daryl Williams, who stutters and you can see in his eyes how much it hurts just to try and say hello, or that girl who moved here last year and you can hardly tell she's breathing she's so afraid of being noticed, but then she keeps drawing these amazing pictures that Mr. Minelli says are "touched by genius." In other words: people who are misfits because they're just who they are instead of "fits," who are like everybody else.

Anyway, I do not want you thinking that I or Addie or Joe or Skeezie feel sorry for ourselves. We do not. Other people may call us names or think we're weird or whatever, but that does not mean we believe them. We may be misfits, but we're okay. Leastwise, in our own eyes we are, and that's all that really matters.

Addie is the one who got us all together. Of course, Addie and I were actually "together" since before either of us can remember because our moms were best friends when we were born, so we became best friends, too. Then Joe moved in next door to Addie when we were four. As for Skeezie, well, I didn't think he'd have *any* friends, the way he was. In kindergarten, he got labeled a troublemaker right off the bat and everybody just kind of knew to steer clear of him; at least, you did if you didn't want a chunk of your hair cut off when you weren't looking or a gob of paste shoved down your underpants.

It was Addie who decided in the second grade that what Skeezie needed was a friend. She sent him a secret Valentine. It said, "I think you are nice even if you act like a moron." Skeezie did not know what "moron" meant. He thought it was a compliment. So he announced in front of the whole class, "If whoever wrote this Valentine tells me who they are, I will give them a dollar."

Before Miss Haskell could shush the class and tell Skeezie he would do no such thing, Addie had her hand in the air and said, "I wrote it." Of course, so did every other kid in the class because we all wanted the dollar. But Addie proved she was telling the truth by providing a sample of her handwriting and Miss Haskell believed her and Skeezie believed her and— here's the part nobody could believe—he did not cut off any of her hair or paste any of her clothing to any of her body parts. He gave her the dollar, and they became friends.

From that day on, Skeezie stopped making trouble. Just like that. Cold turkey. And even though he still acts a little tough and dresses like a fugitive from *West Side Story,* he is at heart the kind of person your mother wants you to be friends with. And all on account of Addie.

Addie has always been like that. If she believes something, she does not keep it inside her head like private property with a NO TRESPASSING sign up; she puts it out there in the world and says, "Deal with it." She is not afraid of anything. Not even the names people call her.

On Monday of the second week of school, she strikes again, this time in Ms. Wyman's homeroom. Ms. Wyman is the seventh-grade math teacher. She is also a believer in the religion of Self-Esteem. Her room is plastered with these signs that say things like, TODAY IS THE FIRST DAY OF THE REST OF YOUR LIFE and IF YOU DON'T BELIEVE IN YOURSELF, WHO WILL? She keeps fresh flowers on her desk and she likes to start each day with these deep yoga breaths so we'll all be "centered" and "at our best." She's so sweet sometimes you swear you can smell muffins baking. But here is the bad news about Ms. Wyman: If you cross her, watch out. That smiley face of hers'll fall off like a mask that's popped its elastic, and underneath is a dragon lady. And *that* Ms. Wyman, I swear, wouldn't blink at removing your liver with her bare hands and eating it with a spoon.

So it is particularly nervy of Addie to do what she does, it being in Ms. Wyman's homeroom and only the second week of school and all.

"We will now stand and say the Pledge of Allegiance."

Some sixth-grade voice I do not recognize is giving the morning announcements over the P.A. Ms. Wyman looks mildly annoyed to have her morning yoga breaths interrupted, but she smiles indulgently at the box on the wall and says, "Boys and girls, please rise."

We do.

"I pledge allegiance to the flag of the United States of . . ."

It is then I notice that not *all* of us has risen. One of us is sitting with her hands folded on her desk and a new look for a new day resting comfortably on her face.

"Addie Carle," Ms. Wyman says after the rest of us finish and sit down.

"Yes, Ms. Wyman?"

"Would you care to tell the class why you did not rise and say the Pledge of Allegiance with us this morning?"

"Yes, Ms. Wyman." Addie takes a deep breath. "I looked the word 'pledge' up in the dictionary and it said—"

"Furniture polish," Kevin Hennessey mutters. A bunch of boys around him laugh, Jimmy Lemon loudest of all.

Ms. Wyman furrows her brow. "Continue, Addie," she says.

"It said, well, it actually said lots of things because the word 'pledge' has multiple meanings, as many words do, but as best I could make out, the meaning that applied to the Pledge of Allegiance was this."

She lifts a piece of paper from her desk and reads, "'Pledge: A promise or agreement by which one binds himself to do or forbear something.'"

She clears her throat.

"Now, besides the fact that the dictionary is hopelessly sexist and it should have said 'himself or herself...'"

Somebody says, "Here goes Know-It-All."

Addie presses on. "Well, admittedly, what is *pledged* is allegiance—or loyalty—to one's country. But isn't there the implication of a promise of liberty and justice for all? And do we have liberty and justice for all in this country? I think not."

She casts her eye on DuShawn Carter, who conveniently is seated to her right and even more conveniently is African-American.

"Addie," Ms. Wyman says. "I think perhaps—"

"Did you happen to read this morning's *New York Times?*" Addie continues. I make a mental note to tell Addie later about my liver-eating theory in regards to Ms. Wyman and to suggest that it might be best not to interrupt her.

"Well, my parents subscribe to *The New York Times*," Addie says, to the accompaniment of groans, "and it's a good thing they do. Otherwise, I wouldn't know half of what's going on in the world. Have you *seen* what is happening in the *unfair* metropolis of New York? You cannot be a black man and walk down the streets of that city without the word 'guilty' stamped on your forehead. The police arrest you—or worse—just because of the color of your skin. I do not call that liberty and—"

"Miss Carle—"

"Ms. Wyman, I will *not* utter empty words, falsehoods, and lies." Addie walks to the front of the room and dramatically presents Ms. Wyman with a piece of paper on which she's neatly penned her dictionary definition of the word "pledge," along with a torn-out page of the newspaper.

Returning to her seat, she says, "I rest my case."

Sitting, she lets out a gigantic fart and turns bright red. Pretty much everybody cracks up. I am sticking the sharp point of my compass into my thumb to keep from laughing because, after all, Addie is one of my best friends.

"Kevin Hennessey!" Ms. Wyman exclaims. I'm sure she figures it is Kevin who put the whoopee cushion on Addie's chair, because statistically speaking— and statistics are Ms. Wyman's raison d'être (which is French for "reason to be," in case not knowing what something means in another language gets in the way of your following the action)—you'd have a pretty good bet that Kevin is guilty of just about anything that happens in school. Anything of a subversive or out-and-out nasty nature, that is. Once Skeezie retired as School Bad Boy, Kevin took over the job. But I have the feeling it isn't Kevin this time. No, I have the feeling it is Addie's Living, Breathing Symbol of Social Injustice who has placed the whoopee cushion on her chair. I mean, DuShawn Carter is laughing so hard he is pretty near busting a gut.

EVERY FRIDAY after school since the beginning of sixth grade, Addie, Joe, Skeezie, and I have gathered at the Candy Kitchen, last booth on the right—the one with the aforementioned torn red leatherette seats— to discuss important issues and eat ice cream. We call this the Forum. Due to the change in my employment status, we canned holding the Forum on a specific day of the week and decided we'd have it whenever we felt like it. The Friday Forum became the Floating Forum.

The minutes of the First Floating Forum of the Seventh-Grade Year are as follows:

Addie: Today's topic for discussion is "Liberty and Justice for All."

Skeezie: Do you have to write down every single word?

Addie: Talk more slowly, please.

Skeezie: Geesh.

Addie: Well, I guess we all know what happened in Ms. Wyman's homeroom class this morning.

Joe: You told us at lunch.

Skeezie: It is all you talked about at lunch.

Joe: Wait a minute, did you write my name down as Joe?

Addie: That is your name, the last I heard.

Joe: Not anymore. Now it's Scorpio.

Skeezie: Scorpio?!

Joe: You should talk, with a name like Skeezie.

Bobby: What happened to Jodan?

Joe: Oh, that putting-my-first-and-middle-names-together thing? That is sooo last week. I like Scorpio. It has, oh, I don't know, energy.

Skeezie: How about Plunger?

Joe: Plunger?

Skeezie:	Yeah, like in toilet plunger. You get one of those things working, man, talk about energy.
Joe:	Wait a minute, I think I hear someone laughing. Oops, my mistake, that was someone gagging in the next booth.
Skeezie:	Ha.
Addie:	Excuse me, could we get back to the topic?
Joe:	Could you write my name as Scorpio?
Addie:	Okay, fine.
Scorpio:	Thank you.
Addie:	You're welcome. Now, what I want to know is if you guys think there is liberty and justice for all in this country.
Scorpio:	No way.
Bobby:	Well, I think what the Pledge of Allegiance is about is idealism. You know, like, what we aim for.
Addie:	But that's not what is says. It says promise.
Bobby:	Where? It doesn't say that word.

Addie: Well, pledge, promise, same thing. The
            point is—

Scorpio: The point is there's no way there is freedom
            and justice for everybody in this country.
            It's, well, I don't mean it's like a total, you
            know, a totalism kind of thing, whatever
            it's called.

Addie: Totalitarianism.

Scorpio: Yeah, that. I mean, it's not like we've got
            some dictator guy telling everybody they
            have to, I don't know, like, wear polyester all
            the time or something grotesque like that.

Skeezie: Oh, yeah, there's a fate worse than death.
            Synthetics.

Addie: I think we're getting a little off the—

Bobby: It's cool that you're not saying the Pledge,
            Addie, I mean it's cool that you're standing
            up for your principles and all, but—

Addie: Thank you.

Bobby: But what difference does it make? I mean,
            just because you sit there and don't say the
            words with everybody else, that's not going

to help some poor guy hundreds of miles downstate in New York City who gets beaten up just because he's black or poor or something.

Addie: I contend that it does make a difference.

Skeezie: Oo, she contends. Where's our food, if you don't mind my asking?

Addie: Yes, I contend that every act of conscience makes a difference.

Skeezie: But you're talking about New York City. We don't have the same kinds of problems here.

Scorpio: Hello. Are you kidding? Of course we do.

Addie: Just on a smaller scale. It's important to bring attention—

Bobby: My dad says it's better just to get along, not make waves. He says bringing attention can be a dangerous thing.

Addie: Of course it can! Just look at Abraham Lincoln or Martin Luther King or . . . or . . .

Scorpio: Madonna. Or RuPaul.

Addie: I don't think they're in quite the same league, Joe. I mean, Scorpio.

Scorpio: They bring attention! They're like, "In your
           face, world! Look at me! This is who I am
           and if you don't like it, stuff it! I'm as good
           as anybody else!"

Skeezie: Tell it!

Bobby: Whatever. The thing is, Ms. Wyman is not
           going to let you not say the Pledge, Addie,
           so what is the point?

Addie: Excuse me? I do not believe Ms. Wyman has
           the right to tell me what I can and cannot
           say. Have you never heard of the First
           Amendment?

Skeezie: Has that bozo who took our order never
           heard of first come, first served? Did you see
           that? He just gave them their food and they
           came in here after we did!

Bobby: Maybe they're friends of his.

Skeezie: There you are, Addie, a perfect example
           of how there's no liberty and justice
           for all. In a just world, I'd be slurping my
           Dr Pepper by now and instead I'm sitting
           here parched and deprived because

Mr. HellomynameisAdam is giving
preferential treatment to his friends.
Justice, I say! Justice!

Addie: Skeezie, stop pounding on the table. You're
making a scene.

Skeezie: Justice! Justice!

Bobby: I thought you wanted to bring attention,
Addie.

Addie: There's bringing attention and then
there's bringing attention. I mean, a
little kid throwing a tantrum in public is
bringing attention and that's closer to
what Skeezie's doing right now than my
standing up for—

Scorpio: I was just thinking. RuPaul. I really like the
sound of that. I think I'm going to be Jodan
again. Except I'll make the "D" capital, so
you have to, like, emphasize the second
syllable, you know? Jo-<u>Dan.</u>

Addie: What are you talking about?

Scorpio: No, no, don't write Scorpio, write . . .

Addie: Oh, I get it. Okay.

JoDan: Yeah, like that. That's cool.

Skeezie: I thought that was so last week.

JoDan: With a small "d." That was so last week.

Skeezie: Right, whatever.

Addie: So about liberty and justice for—

Skeezie: All right! Here's our food. See, a little
            protest'll work every time. You were right,
            Addie! It pays to act on your conscience.
            Hey, I learned something today. These
            Forums are way cool. Hey, hey, wait a
            minute.

Hellomy
nameis
Adam: What's wrong?

Skeezie: This Dr Pepper is flat, my man. You gotta get
            me another.

Hellomy
nameis
Adam: Look . . .

Skeezie: Justice! Justice!

Hellomy
nameis
Adam: All right, all right. Just cool your jets,
            will you?

Skeezie: Peace, brother.

We do not record the rest of the proceedings, since we never do get back on the topic. If I recall correctly, we spend the rest of our time at the Candy Kitchen that Monday talking about who are the meanest teachers in seventh grade and who are the best. Ms. Wyman scores points in both categories.

TUESDAY MORNING, we get to school, and what do we find scrawled in big ugly marker on Joe's locker but the word Fagot.

Joe is outraged.

"Don't they teach *spelling* in this school?" he goes, then yells across the hall to Kevin Hennessey, who is wearing his usual smirk, "There are two 'g's in 'faggot,' you numbskull!"

"*I* didn't do it!" Kevin shouts back. "Not this time, anyways."

"Yeah, well, tell your illiterate friends that if they're going to call names, they should at least know how to spell them."

"Okay, f-a-i-r-y," Kevin retorts with an evil grin.

Joe gives him the raspberry.

"Liver pâté," I mutter under my breath, which is

code for: Ms. Wyman should rip his liver out, toss it in a blender, and serve it on crackers.

Joe and Kevin have been doing this little dance together since kindergarten when Kevin told the whole class that Joey didn't have a pee-pee and Joe announced in a loud voice that he had *two* pee-pees and Kevin was just jealous.

"Faggot," Kevin Hennessey spits as the bell rings.

"Numbskull of Unknown Paternal Origin," Joe spits back.

"Good one," I say.

Kevin jabs Joe with his elbow, then goes, "Out of the way, Lardbar," to me as he pushes his way into Ms. Wyman's homeroom. Joe rolls his eyes at me and shrugs before moving down the hall to Mr. Daly's homeroom. Just another morning at Paintbrush Falls Middle School.

Now, as my classmates and I settle into our seats (we have at least a couple of minutes before Ms. Wyman leads us in yoga breathing), let me tell you about the first time I laid eyes on Joe. He was four. So was I.

I and my mom were visiting Addie and her mom,

when Addie ups and tells me I should go check out the new kid next door. I noticed she did not offer to go with me.

"Just ring the bell," she told me.

So I did. When the inside door opened, there on the other side of the screen was this kid wearing a dress.

"Will you marry me?" the kid in the dress asked.

I shook my head.

"Why?"

"I am going to marry my mother," I answered. My mother did not yet know this.

"Can I marry your mother, too?"

"No."

"Can I marry your father?"

"No."

"Can you play with me?"

"Okay," I said.

"I'm Joe," he said.

"Okay."

"I'm a boy," he told me, lifting his dress to show me the proof. He was not wearing underpants. (For the record, he had only one pee-pee.)

"I never knew a boy who wore a dress," I told him.

"There's a lot you don't know," he said.

He was right about that.

It wasn't the last time Joe wore a dress. He kept taking stuff from his mother's closet and trying it on until his mother finally gave him his own box filled with clothes she was through with and he could dress up to his heart's content.

He doesn't wear dresses anymore—at least, not that I'm aware of—but lately he's taken to running a streak of color through his hair and he's always got the nail of his right pinky finger painted some crazy way. Sometimes his aunt Pam, who sells cosmetics at Awkworth & Ames but is really an artist, paints these tiny pictures on it. Faces or flowers or symbols. They're pretty amazing. Even Kevin Hennessey has been known to say, "Cool." Right now, there's a scorpion on his finger, on account of his being Scorpio, I guess, except that's changed of course and he's JoDan, but I never remember to call him any of these names *du jour* anyway and just call him Joe.

As for Pam, well, I'll have to tell you more about her later on, because we're halfway through home-

34

room period and I perhaps should listen up in case Ms. Wyman says something that might be of actual use. I do want to tell you this, though: Pam is beautiful. I don't mean ordinary Paintbrush Falls beautiful; I mean, like from a whole other planet beautiful. And although she does not smile all the time (she's no phony), when she does, she's got the kind of smile that makes your chest feel two sizes too small and your brain two sizes too big, and the truth is I can hardly stand being around her most of the time. Or at least my body can hardly stand it.

". . . elections three weeks from today," I hear Ms. Wyman saying. I had best tune us back into the action because these elections she is going on about are going to play a big part in this story—and, although I have no way of knowing this at this moment, they will play an even bigger part in the story of my life.

"As you will recall, you all registered as Democrats or Republicans in the sixth grade—"

"Or Independents," Addie pipes up.

Ms. Wyman gives Addie a look that's laced with arsenic, on account of being interrupted.

"Or Independents," she gives. "Now, anyone interested in running for student council on either ticket has until Thursday, seventh period, when the nominating conventions will take place—Republicans in the auditorium, Democrats in the media center."

Out of the corner of my eye I see Addie stir. I want to swat her with a rolled-up newspaper, but I do not have a rolled-up newspaper and besides I remind myself she is not a fly.

"Where will the Independents meet?" she asks, to which Kevin goes, "The girls' john," and general hilarity ensues.

Ms. Wyman brings this to an abrupt halt with threats of detention or disembowelment, I have trouble hearing which.

"We have a two-party system," she says firmly, once order has been restored.

"But—"

"The candidates from the *two* parties will meet with me, as student council adviser, in this room after school on Thursday. Any questions?"

Addie raises her hand.

"Good," Ms. Wyman snaps, grabbing a stack of papers from her desk. "Then we can move on. Brittney, would you pass these out, please?"

Brittney Hobson jumps up. "I'd be happy to," she says perkily. Brittney is the kind of person for whom active verbs and modifiers were invented.

As we read about the seventh-grade dance coming up in October, the announcements come on the P.A., and soon we are standing for the Pledge.

Or not.

Which explains why Ms. Wyman now has that liver-eating look on her face and is saying to Addie, "Miss Carle, I think perhaps you had best go see Mr. Kiley."

Some of the boys go, "Oooo."

"That's enough!" snaps Ms. Wyman. "Miss Carle, you may be excused."

Addie rises to her full height, meaning she occupies all the vertical space she's entitled to instead of slumping, which she sometimes does because of her being so tall and getting called names on account of it, and she walks to the door, clutching her books. When she gets there, she turns and cradles the books

in the crook of her left arm and raises her right hand
high in the air so she looks, I swear on a stack of pancakes, like the spitting image of the Statue of Liberty
(which I expect is exactly what she intends) and she
proclaims in a voice that sounds like she's been listening a whole lot of times to that "I Have a Dream"
speech: "Until there is LIBERTY and JUSTICE for
AWWLL . . . let there be TRUTH in SILENCE!"

Ms. Wyman's jaw drops. Some of the kids clap.
Some laugh. Jimmy Lemon calls out, "What a loser!"
Ms. Wyman says, "That will be enough, Mr. Lemon."
DuShawn Carter sends a spitball flying, but it misses
Addie because she's turned and walked out, and hits
the "a" in Ms. Wyman's name on the door instead.
Ms. Wyman sees it and there's blood in her eyes as
she yells, "Kevin Hennessey!"

"Why is it always me!" Kevin protests. "I didn't
do it!"

The whole class gets laughing so hard I forget that
Addie is in serious trouble.

5

SO NOW it is Tuesday after school and an emergency meeting of the Forum has been called on account of what happened to Addie today, her being sent to Mr. Kiley's office and all, as well as some other matters I will attend to in due course. But I am not yet sitting with Addie and Skeezie and Joe in the back booth with the torn red leatherette upholstery at the Candy Kitchen; as of this very moment I am standing ten feet away from Killer Man, waiting. I listen to the sound of his fingertips drumming the wooden edge of the Calvin Klein neckwear display case, while at the same time making the observation that whenever the Muzak choral *oo-ah* rendition of "Raindrops Keep Falling on my Head" plays it is always followed by a sprightly accordion version of "Y.M.C.A.," and I think I may be trapped in a time warp or an episode of *The*

Twilight Zone. And then I begin to worry that if I keep coming here on Tuesdays and Fridays and the occasional Saturdays, I will become accustomed to standing around waiting for customers who do not appear, waiting for time to pass, waiting for who knows what, and that eventually I will turn into either Mr. Kellerman or a Zen Buddhist.

I do not know why I have this job, except that my dad does not make much money at the nursery and I do what I can to help out. So, okay, I know I have to work, but why *this* job, I cannot figure, other than that my dad knows the store manager. Perhaps, I think, it is not about the job. Perhaps there is a lesson I am meant to glean from the experience. Perhaps it will make me a better person. I think, *I am already turning into a Zen Buddhist.*

At this moment, the anti-Buddha walks in, in the person of JoDan Bunch.

"Look at you," he greets me with, "in that tie with all the little amoebas on it. How science dweeb is *that?*"

"These aren't amoebas," I inform him. "This a style called paisley."

"Well, I think I knew that," says Joe, casting his eyes over the ties on the nearest display table and gingerly selecting a purple one. At least I do not have to worry that his hands are filthy. This is never a question with Joe.

I glance over my shoulder to see if Killer Man is giving me the evil oculus, but he is not so much as looking in my direction. He appears to be lost in thought and whatever has got his brain cells occupied is having a strange effect on his facial muscles. They are not locked into their usual the-world-is-beneath-me sneer, but hang on his face like melting cheese, creating the illusion that he is an actual human being and a sad one, at that. Seeing him like this makes me wonder once again about his life outside of Awkworth & Ames, and I make a mental note to try and find out a thing or two.

Joe has come to remind me of the emergency Forum at five-fifteen, which will be brief but crucial. I have no doubt that the words coming out of his mouth have been supplied by Addie. Joe does not say such things as "brief but crucial," whereas Addie loves to make herself sound like a business executive. I worry about her sometimes.

Joe has also come to have his pinky fingernail repainted by his aunt Pam.

"Can you take a break?" he asks me.

I look at the clock. I have been working (or what passes for working at Awkworth & Ames) for only forty minutes. I am not entitled to a break until I have worked for at least an hour. It says that somewhere in the six stapled pages.

"Not yet," I tell him.

Joe goes off to find his aunt Pam. He is doing a little dance as he goes that is a sort of polka version of "Y.M.C.A." and I return to listening to Mr. Kellerman's digit-drumming and I suddenly imagine I hear this deep voice intoning, "You are traveling to another dimension, a dimension not only of sight and sound but of mind. Your next stop, the Twilight Zone!"

My dad and I have been watching *way* too many episodes of *The Twilight Zone*.

By the time my break comes and I join up with Joe, Pam has already finished painting his finger-

nail with a black-and-white yin-yang sign on a bright
yellow background.

"Like it?" Joe asks. This is *not* a multiple-choice
question.

"Awesome," I say.

Pam is standing there, with her hair all frosted
pink to match the pink jacket they make all the cosmetics ladies at Awkworth & Ames wear. On most of
them, it looks like a rag—a *shmatte,* Joe calls it—but
on her it's high fashion. I get a sniff of some kind of
perfume I'd bet a week's supply of Mallomars has the
word "magnolia" somewhere in its name, and I decide
that the only way I can handle a conversation at the
moment without embarrassing myself is to select a
boring topic.

My topic of choice: Killer Man.

"Hey, Pam," I say, trying to sound old and studly.

"Hey, Bobby," she gives back in a magnolia sort of
way, making me feel I've almost succeeded.

"What do you know about Mr. Kellerman?" I go on,
figuring the faster we get to the boring stuff the better
for all concerned.

Pam laughs. At the sound of it, I pray, *Dear God, give me the strength to get through the next ten minutes without dissolving into a pool of lustful preteen sweat.*

"Funny question," Pam says.

"Bobby's a funny guy," Joe puts in. "Oo."

When Joe goes, "Oo," it usually means he has found something more interesting going on than his conversation with you, so do not expect further attention. In this case, what distracts him is an Estée Lauder gift bag that is your gift with any twenty-five-dollar purchase. Joe *has* to know what's in it. He moves down the counter to check it out.

Pam leans on her elbows in my direction, a move that causes me to develop an intense, nearly scientific interest in my shoelaces.

"Mr. Kellerman," she says. "Hm. Well, he's kind of a sad character, isn't he?"

I notch my head about one degree Pam's way. "You think?" I ask. "He seems kind of that way to me today, too. But most times he just seems like the kind of person who never learned to get up on the right side of the bed."

44

Pam laughs again and my sweat glands go into overdrive. I curse whoever invented adolescence and ask God to keep me upright and odor-free for another eight minutes.

"He's a real grouch, for sure," she goes on. "But one thing I've learned in my twenty-eight years of living, Bobby, is that if somebody's a grouch, it's usually because they're not happy. And if they're not happy, there's a reason for it."

"So do you know what the reason is in Kellerman's case?" I am aware I am not calling him Killer Man in front of Pam. I do not want her to think lowly of me.

Pam says, "All I know is that he's a middle-aged guy who still lives with his mother and gets up every day of his life to sell clothes in a department store untouched by the passage of time. That would be enough to make *me* a grouch. Why the interest?"

I shrug. It's the best answer I have.

"Well, if you're like me," Pam goes, letting me off the hook, "you're curious what makes people tick. I mean, we're all so complicated, don't you think? Sometimes, I think we're *too* complicated. That's why

I came *here* to live for a while. Simplify things, you know?"

I nod like I know what she's talking about. I do not have a clue.

"Mr. Goodspeed!"

"Gotta go," I say, and make a mad dash for the men's department.

From the sound of his voice Killer Man is back to being his old cranky self. The trouble is, now that I've heard what Pam has to say about him, I can't see him as 100% cranky anymore, or 100% terrible, or 100% anything except maybe 100% human and I'm not so sure I like that. Because when you get down to it, thinking of somebody as 100% human seriously gets in the way of hating them.

6

Bobby: Thanks for waiting for me, you guys. So what's today's topic?

Addie: "Popularity versus Principles."

Bobby: O-ka-ay. I'm going to need serious ice cream to deal with that one. Double-double chocolate.

Addie: Is that a good idea? You're going to have dinner when you get home. Your dad will kill you if you fill up on ice cream.

Bobby: Yes, Wendy.

Addie: What?

Bobby: Wendy and the Lost Boys.

Addie: Oh. Well, that fits, doesn't it?

Skeezie: Speak for yourselves. I personally am not lost.

JoDan: Guffaw.

Addie: May I have your attention, children?

Bobby,
Skeezie
& JoDan: Yes, Wendy.

Addie: Very funny. Now, I called this emergency
            meeting because of the elections.

Skeezie: Wait, I never heard what happened with
            Kiley.

JoDan: How come you weren't at lunch today?

Skeezie: I had a date with Mrs. DePaolo. I was givin'
            her tongue.

JoDan: That is sooo gross.

Skeezie: Uh-uh. It was tasty.

Addie: Shut up!

Bobby: You're a sick man, Skeezie.

Addie: Can we be serious?

JoDan: You're always serious, Addie. Seriously.

Addie: I am not.

JoDan: Are so.

Skeezie: Yeah, yeah. So what happened, anyways?

Addie: Okay, let's see. Mr. Kiley told me I was
            within my rights not to say the Pledge, but
            that he personally had a hard time with my
            position because he fought for this country
            in an unpopular war.

Skeezie: For the North or the South?

JoDan: Not the Civil War, dummy. The Vietnam War.
           Right?

Addie: Right.

Skeezie: I think I knew that. I was making a joke.

JoDan: Duh.

Addie: Ahem. Anyway, he said that the Pledge
           means a lot to <u>some</u> people and that <u>other</u>
           people don't appreciate all that this country
           is and how great a democratic nation we are
           and blah-blah-blah. But when I tried to
           argue the point about our not being <u>such</u> a
           democratic nation as he contends we are,
           well, he wasn't very interested in hearing
           that. All of a sudden, he had an important
           meeting he just <u>had</u> to go to and he was,
           like, whisking me out the door, as if I'd let
           off a stink bomb in his office and he was
           going to have to have it fumigated. Anyway,
           he told me he would inform Ms. Wyman that
           while I did not have to say the Pledge, I
           should stand up out of respect for my fellow
           classmates.

Skeezie: Are you going to?

Addie: I guess. I mean, what I'm really objecting to
          are the <u>words</u>, not standing or sitting.
          Although I can't say I like being told I <u>have</u>
          to stand up. I mean, I am <u>not</u> a robot.

JoDan: You go, girl.

Addie: So about the elections.

Skeezie: If the service gets much slower in this place,
          I swear I'm gonna take a job here myself, just
          so's I can get something to eat. Who's workin'
          today? Oh, no, it's HellomynameisEric. He's
          even worse than HellomynameisAdam.

Addie: The student council elections are going to be
          in three weeks, so we have to get going on
          this right away.

JoDan: We?

Bobby: Get going with what?

Addie: I want us to form a new party. The Freedom
          Party.

Bobby: Ms. Wyman said there are two parties and
          <u>only</u> two parties, and, anyway, Brittney's
          going to win.

JoDan: Oo, Brittney "Aren't I Fabulous?" Hobson.

Addie: She's not so bad.

JoDan: Brittney "All the Boys Like Me, I'm so
          Popular I Could Die" Hobson.

Addie: Joe!

Bobby: But that's the point. She is popular. She
          wins everything she runs for.

Addie: Big deal, she was elected class president for
          the past three years. But this is the student
          council, the governing body of the whole
          middle school.

Skeezie: I can't believe you want to compete with her.

Addie: It's not about competing with her.

JoDan: Brittney "Miss Future Anorexic Cheerleader
          Prom Queen My Life Will Be Over at
          Seventeen" Hobson.

Addie: Look, that's why today's topic is "Popularity
          versus Principles." What I want to know is:
          If there's a contest between somebody who's
          really popular—okay, let's say Brittney—

Skeezie: Just for the sake of argument.

Addie: And somebody who isn't popular but stands

for Truth and Freedom and Liberty for All,
do you think the person who stands for
Truth and Freedom and Liberty for All has
a chance of winning?

JoDan: In your dreams.

Skeezie: No way.

Bobby: Uh-uh. Popularity wins. Period.

Addie: What a bunch of cynics!

Skeezie: We calls it likes we sees it, babe.

Addie: I will overlook the sexism.

Skeezie: I was thinking of the pig of book and movie
fame actually. No, no, put the salt down! Oh,
man, I'll never get this out of my hair!

Addie: Perhaps if you didn't use so much mousse . . .

Bobby: Here are our sodas.

Skeezie: 'Bout time.

Addie: Okay, fair is fair. I did ask your opinion and
you're probably right. So I won't run for
president. But I <u>could</u> run for vice president.

Skeezie: Yeah, nobody cares who the vice president
is. Nobody even knows who the vice
president is.

JoDan: So who's going to be your candidate for president? Oh, please tell me it's Tonni. Don't you just love her hair? She has the most fabulous hair. And that name: Tondayala Cherise DuPré. Just saying it is like eating dessert, don't you think? But not like a heavy dessert—and not too sweet. No, no. Light and airy. Lemon chiffon pie, with a dollop of whipped cream.

Bobby: Stop it, Joe, you're killing me.

JoDan: Why she insists on being called Tonni is beyond me. I mean, I would die for a name like hers. She'd win, you know. She's really popular and sooo beautiful. And she knows how to put herself together, which is important in a politician these days. I mean, it's all about image. And she's—

Skeezie: Black.

JoDan: Well, there is that.

Addie: My thinking exactly.

Skeezie: You want Tonni to run for president because she's black?

Addie:	Of course not. Besides, she's got way too much attitude.
JoDan:	Attitude is what it's all about. Trust me, Addie, I know about stuff like this. I speak celebrity.
Addie:	Stop, JoDan. It scares me how shallow you are. Anyway, who I'm thinking of is DuShawn.
JoDan:	DuShawn Carter?
Skeezie:	No, DuShawn Feingold. How many DuShawns are there?
Bobby:	But how do you know he'd <u>want</u> to run for president?
Addie:	I don't. We'll have to convince him.
Skeezie:	Oh, this will be good. The four biggest misfits in school are going to convince one of the most popular kids in school—not to mention the High Exalted Emperor of Spitballs— that he should be <u>our</u> candidate for student council president. This is not going to happen.
Addie:	I contend it will.

Skeezie: What's going to convince him, if you don't mind my asking?

Addie: The truth, that's what will convince him. That, and the opportunity to be taken seriously. Nobody takes DuShawn seriously. I don't know if he takes himself seriously. He's smart, but he acts like a goof-off.

Skeezie: That's because he _is_ a goof-off.

Addie: Well, we're giving him a chance to be more than a goof-off.

Skeezie: But you're picking him because he's popular _and_, excuse me for pointing it out—_again_— because he's black.

Addie: Both of which factors will help advance our cause.

Bobby: Which is?

Addie: Freedom. Truth. Justice for All.

Skeezie: You forgot salt.

Addie: What? Oh, no, don't you dare! Skeezie, put that saltshaker down!

Skeezie: Justice for all, Addie, justice for all!

7

ONE OF the nice things about living in a little town like Paintbrush Falls is that you can walk or bike just about anyplace you might be of a mind to go. If it so happens you're *not* of a mind to go someplace, well, there are only so many long-ways-around before you end up there anyway. It may also be the last town in these United States of America where nobody bothers much about locked doors or wondering where their kids are. If they're not at home, you can bet on a stack of pancakes that they are within yoo-hooing distance of somebody who knows them.

For characters like Skeezie and me, a town this size is a perfect fit; at least, that's the way it feels to me at the age of twelve. For others—Addie and Joe coming to mind—Paintbrush Falls is a tight squeeze at best, and the more years that go by the more that characters like this will be eager to try on something bigger. I have my suspicions that both Addie and Joe will be looking for something a *lot* bigger, something that will give them plenty of wiggle room while they try and figure out who they are and what they want to do with the rest of their lives.

Well, as I am on my meander home from that last Forum meeting, of which the topic was "Popularity versus Principles," I am in a philosophical frame of thinking. But it isn't small-town living or even popularity versus principles that occupies my mind, so much as it is justice. Justice for all.

Addie feels that everyone should be entitled to everything. That is the American way, she says. But I look all around me and I see people wanting just a little piece of something, not the whole pie, and coming up shortchanged even then, and I do not see them being cheated out of their rights. I just see them being dealt a hand. Some people get a royal flush and some get a pair of deuces. And some people get nothing but a string of cards that no matter how they're played will never add up to a winning hand.

I guess who I am thinking about mostly is my dad.

When I walk in the door I can smell the onions frying and I know my dad is making one of his whatever's-on-the-bottom-shelf-of-the-refrigerator stir-fries. These are not bad and besides anything goes with ketchup.

"Hey, Skip," he greets me with, and I do not mind this, despite the fact that this nickname originated in the same era as "Fluff." As I told you way back on another page, I was called "Fluff" because of my fondness for peanut butter and Marshmallow Fluff sandwiches. My dad, feeling sorry for me at the time, gives me the at-home nickname of "Skippy," in honor of my peanut butter of choice. Over time, I prefer "Skip" to "Skippy," and "Skip" it is. But this is just a nickname between my dad and me, not for the outside world, in the same vein as my calling him "Hammer." "Hammer" is on account of him liking detective stories and his name being Mike, and when I discover that Mike Hammer is his detective of choice at the time I am about seven or eight, well, I give him that moniker and it sticks.

I am recalling that at around that same time is when he also starts in reading me Damon Runyon stories every night at bedtime and this has a lasting effect on me. Like, for instance, the way I just used "moniker" for "nickname." If you don't know who Damon Runyon is—and why would you, seeing as how *your* dad was reading you *The House at Pooh Corner* while mine was dishing out "All Horse Players Die Broke"—well, he was this fellow who wrote stories about these great low-life characters with monikers like Harry the Horse and Milk-Ear Willie and some of these characters made it into a musical called *Guys and Dolls*—and surely you have heard of *that*.

My dad was a bit of a low-life character himself in those days. I remember more than once his having a glass of scotch in one hand whilst he was reading me from a book with the other. Those were hard days and hard nights. My dad almost did not survive them, I think, and when I get that thought going in my head, it gives me the willies, and I have to do something fast to wake up to the here and now and see that he did survive, and he no longer has a glass of scotch in his hands or any other kind of liquid poison that will cause him to be crying out in the middle of the night with me sitting up in my bed on the other side of the wall, listening and shaking so hard I think I'm going to be sick, but all it is, is I'm scared.

"How was work, Skip?" he asks me before he inquires about school. I think he is nervous I am going to hate my job so much I won't want to stick it out. And, like I say, we need the money. We are not dirt poor, but we do not live in a fancy house, not that the house we lived in before my mom died was so fancy or anything, but it was a few rungs up the ladder from the trailer we have called home for the past few years. We are saving what we can to fix this place up or maybe even get a house again, but it's only been a couple of years that my dad has been working nice and steady, so I do what I can to help out.

Do not get me wrong. I am not a snob. I have no problem with living in a trailer. I figure it is just one of the cards my dad and I have been dealt.

I tell him work was fine. I do not go into particulars, such as that I did nothing but stand around for two hours, except for maybe fifteen minutes of helping Mr. Kellerman rearrange tie displays that did not need rearranging. "Fine" is all I say, and "fine" is all it is he needs to hear.

"How was work for you today?" I ask then, and "fine" is what he gives back. I can tell that he has had a hard day at the nursery so I settle into doing my homework, leaving further discussion to a time when he has a mind for it.

My dad wanted to have his own nursery once, but all he does is work in one. He's lucky to be doing that, as he reminds me every time, my guess is, he needs to remind himself.

At dinner that night, which is so good I do not even reach for the ketchup, he asks me, after we do the dishes and play a couple of hands of cards, do I want to watch *The Godfather Part II*, which he has rented from the local video establishment. I say sure thing, on account of the first *Godfather* being one of my all-time favorite movies and also because watching old movies with my dad—the classics, he calls them—is one of my all-time favorite things to do.

Still, I can't help pondering how my dad never—with a capital NEVER—goes out. So right then and there, without even thinking about it, I up and ask him if he would like to be a chaperon for the middle-school dance, which is coming up in a few weeks, the same Friday as the student council election. I do not tell him about the election or Addie's plan to start a new party at school and run DuShawn Carter for president, because I know he will start in on Addie's liberal politics and how she is too much of an idealist, like her parents. I am not partial to hearing my dad talk that way, because once he was an idealist and a liberal, too, and he and my mom and Addie's parents were best friends and always working together for one cause or another. But all that changed after my mom died and my dad hit the bad times.

"Hm, chaperon," he says. "Well."

"Yes. Well?"

"I don't know, Skip."

"Aw, come on," I say. "Don't you want to keep your eye on me and my peers as we venture forth into the wonderful world of puberty?"

This one gets a smile out of him.

"What a way with words you got," he says. "Like your mother."

"Yeah, well," I say. "Come on, Dad."

"I'll think about it," he says. "I went to that school, you know."

"Duh."

"I feel funny going back, is all. Not that I haven't been back, but to a dance and all. I don't know, I'll think about it. You really planning to go? You and your friends don't exactly seem the dance-going type, if you don't mind my saying."

"Types change," I go, feeling a little embarrassed because, truth to tell, I'd have to agree with him. But it seems like we do want to go, so maybe I did tell the truth. Maybe types do change.

"Game of casino?" I hear. "We can do the dishes later."

"Sure," I say.

I clear the table. He gets the cards.

"Skip," he says, shuffling.

"Hammer," I give back.

Two tough card sharks squaring off. I can almost picture each of us with a glass of scotch sitting at our right hands. Except that we're both lefties and in about a half hour he'll be saying, "Oreos?"

And we both know there's only one drink of choice with Oreos—and it isn't scotch.

8

BACK AT school, Ms. Wyman is having a hard time going along with Mr. Kiley's instructions to leave Addie be, so long as she stands up with the rest of us. This is because Ms. Wyman is big on rules, which will not surprise you, and one of her rules is: Everybody says the Pledge. I see her giving Addie the evil oculus every morning as Addie stands there, silent as dandruff and every bit as annoying. By Thursday, it looks to me like Ms. Wyman is doing everything she can to keep from hurling herself across the room, scattering innocent seventh graders to the four corners of the earth, and tearing Addie's liver out with her bare teeth.

An exaggeration? I don't think so.

"Ms. Wyman is not a happy person" is all Addie has to say when I point out the effect her actions are having on the teacher formerly known as IF I REACH FOR THE STARS I JUST MIGHT TOUCH THE MOON. (This sign was retired after Ms. Wyman got tired of Kevin Hennessey making jokes about the word "moon.")

It occurs to me that Addie may have a point, which, when I add this to what I know about Mr. Kellerman and even my own father, gets me to wondering if "not a happy person" is part of the definition of "adult."

Ms. Wyman and Addie are also going head-to-head on this third-party business, of course. I suspect that Ms. Wyman would not care so much if she didn't already have it in for Addie on account of the Pledge.

"There is no need for a new political party," Ms. Wyman states flatly Thursday morning in homeroom. "Work within the system, Miss Carle."

"But a third party will give new blood to the system!" Addie protests. Kevin, who is sitting to my right, adds a third drop of red ballpoint blood to the two already oozing off the end of the knife he's drawn on his binder. I try to picture Kevin's future. What comes to mind is a row of numbers across his chest.

"Let's all rise for some deep yoga breaths," Ms. Wyman announces, her voice all of a sudden dripping maple syrup.

Addie goes, "But—" and is cut off by Ms. Wyman intoning, "Breathe innnn."

"Looks like she left you with your 'but' hangin' out," DuShawn cracks, which I am sorry to say I find pretty amusing and get to laughing on account of it right along with Kevin and Jimmy Lemon and the rest of the goofballs.

At lunch that day, Addie says, "Ms. Wyman may hate me, but she can't stop the democratic process."

We're sitting there—Skeezie and Joe and Addie and myself—debating the reason that Skeezie's mother continues to put boxes of raisins in his lunch even after she has been informed that the only purpose they serve before being tossed is to spark debates on the reason she continues to put them in his lunch, when Addie ups and announces, "I am going over there to ask DuShawn to run for president."

And she goes. But not until she says, "Bobby, will you go with me, please?"

I figure she needs my support.

"DuShawwwn," Joe drawls in this dreamy way he gets sometimes. "I never thought about his name before. It's like mine. And RuPaul's. You know—RuPaul, JoDan, DuShawn. Do you think I'm trying to be black?"

"Eat your raisins," Skeezie tells him, tossing the box at him as Addie and I set off on our journey to uncharted territory: the center of the cafeteria.

DuShawn is there, at his usual table in the middle of the action, and with him are Kevin Hennessey, Jimmy Lemon, Royal Wilkins, and Tondayala Cherise DuPré, who most times will be referred to as Tonni, but every once in awhile, I just have to haul out her whole name, because I happen to agree with Joe on this one: A moniker like that is like a peacock with its tail feathers open. You've just got to see it in all its glory.

DuShawn, Tonni, and Royal are the only black students in the seventh grade, and they are partial to hanging out together for this reason. As for Kevin Hennessey and Jimmy Lemon, well, Kevin is a friend of DuShawn's, probably on account of they are both wise guys—as in "Ha-ha," not "Aha!", because *there* they part company: DuShawn's cranium is by far the superior of the two. And Jimmy, well, Jimmy is the kind of guy guys like DuShawn and Kevin need around them. He's the audience.

"DuShawn, I need to talk with you," Addie says.

DuShawn raises an eyebrow about a millimeter. I am impressed by the precision of this and am wondering how long he has practiced it, when he says out of the corner of this mouth, "I'm listening." The theme song of *The Godfather* starts playing in my head. Or is it *The Godfather Part II?*

"Well," says Addie. Nobody invites us to sit. I am just thankful I haven't been called a name yet. "You know that I am starting a new political party. And, don't worry, I'll convince Ms. Wyman. It is my hope to create a voice that will speak to those *without* a voice, to speak out on behalf of the injustices that riddle our society — and P.F.M.S., in particular. Injustices with which I am sure you have personal acquaintance."

"What makes you think that?" DuShawn asks.

Royal giggles. Tonni, who possesses the humor of a clenched fist, stiffens noticeably.

Not picking up on the reaction of the two girls,

Addie shrugs and lets out a little puff of air. "Well, I don't mean to be obvious . . ."

"Oh, that's okay," DuShawn goes on. "You can be obvious with me. Me and my friends here, we're not too bright."

"Speak for yourself," Kevin says, indicating he may have missed the discussion on irony in Language Arts class.

Addie slumps slightly and leans her head in toward DuShawn's. "Being a minority," she goes on, articulating the words dangerously, "you have certainly seen your share of injustice."

DuShawn nods. I back away from the sparks I can feel starting to shoot off the top of Tonni's head. I want to pinch Addie or slink back to my table in the corner, but it is too late. Addie presses on.

"So would you run for president of the student council, DuShawn? On the Freedom Party ticket?"

DuShawn gets this gleam in his eye. "Interesting," he says. "Kind of like me representing freedom. Like freedom from slavery, maybe."

"That's a good point," Addie says. I am beginning

to think she may have missed that discussion on irony, too.

"So I'd be, like, a symbol," DuShawn goes on. I am waiting for Tonni to ignite. It will happen, do not worry about that. "I mean, of course I would be myself, me, DuShawn Carter, human being seventh-grade student and all, but I would also be like a symbol of oppressed peoples everywhere, of, like, all those who are still in bondage, waiting to be freed. Yeah, I could be like the image of, you know, the po' old plantation slave and Abraham Lincoln, all wrapped up in one."

Oh, he is good. He may be the High Exalted Emperor of Spitballs, but this guy has been staying awake in class.

Addie, at last, is starting to get it.

"Well, you may be getting a little carried away, but that *is* the idea, I guess. So will you do it? Oh, and I was thinking maybe I would run for vice president. And, well, the rest of the slate is still open. We could talk about that."

DuShawn rubs his chin. "Well, ah dunno," he says, dropping his voice so low we might have to go looking for it under the table. I see how he's puffing out his lips, and I have a feeling I know where he's headed, so I tap Addie on the arm, just to give her a little warning.

"Ah'm thinkin' dat might be mighty fine, Miz Addie," DuShawn drones. He's really getting into it, pulling at his chin and nodding his head up and down like it belongs on the back window ledge of somebody's car. "Soon's I get in from de cotton field, ah'm gwine to havva give dis a little cogitatin'."

I am impressed. Especially that he remembers a vocabulary word from sixth grade.

Jimmy reaches across the table to high-five DuShawn as Kevin gets to howling so hard he folds right over and mashes his forehead into what's left of his pizza. Royal is laughing, too, but not Tondayala Cherise DuPré. She is sitting there stiff as a comb. I watch her eyeballs swell up and wonder what she's going to say when Addie opens her mouth again. I glance down to see if she's got any more feet left to put in it.

"That's a riot, DuShawn," Addie says. "Disrespecting your ancestors. Really. A laugh riot. I guess I made a mistake thinking anybody would take you seriously when you can't even take yourself—or your own people—seriously. Come on, Bobby, let's not waste any more time."

We start to walk away.

But we don't get far.

"Who you think you're talkin' to?" Tonni's voice lands on our ears with the *thwak* of the morning paper hitting the front door. We stop and turn.

Tonni's up on her feet, hands on her hips, chin thrust out like a dare. DuShawn is standing, too, but the way his baggy pants cascade from hip to floor he looks like a question mark next to Tonni's exclamation point. Addie takes a step in their direction. I follow. The cafeteria goes dead quiet. There isn't a slurp or a crinkle or a crunch anywhere—just our feet hitting the linoleum and Tonni's hard stare, which I swear makes noise. If I could remember the theme song to *Gunfight at the O.K. Corral*, it'd be playing in my head.

"Now you listen here," Tonni spits out as soon as Addie and I are in range. "You got no right talkin' to DuShawn like that, does she, DuShawn?" DuShawn opens his mouth, but all that comes out is nothing. "You hear what I'm telling you? You think you can speak for black people, you think you know what it *is* to be black when what are you but a lily-white girl living your whole life in a lily-white town with a lily-white name like Paintbrush Falls, and you want to start some sort of liberation movement or something and use DuShawn here like some kind of fool pawn or something, like he's gonna make you black or something?"

"This isn't about black or white," Addie says.

"What?" Tonni squeals. "Don't be tellin' me this isn't about black or white. It's *always* about black or white, and if you don't think so, it's because you're white."

A couple of black eighth graders start clapping and shouting, "Right on!" and "You go, sister!" but the rest of us are standing there with our tongues glued to the bottoms of our mouths.

Except Addie.

"Look," she says, "I'm sorry you're angry, Tonni. I guess I'm a little naive about some things . . ."

Tonni snorts. "You *guess! Huh!*"

"But I really think DuShawn would be a good candidate. Everybody likes him and he's funny and he's—"

"Black," says Tonni.

"Does that have to matter?" Addie gives back. "What matters is he's a lot smarter than he lets on. And I just think it's time to take DuShawn Carter seriously."

"Excuse me? You know what you are, Addie? You're one of those do-good liberals come pokin' their white noses into black business, so full of themselves like they *know* what's good for people they know nothin' about. Well, I know a lot more about bein' black than you do, and I know DuShawn a whole lot better than you do, and what DuShawn thinks is—"

"I'll do it," DuShawn puts in.

Addie and Tonni drop dead and stare at him. I can't tell who is more shocked.

"No, it's cool," says DuShawn. "I'll do it."

"DuShawn, you gone outta your fool mind?!" Tonni hollers.

"Thank you," Addie says. "You won't regret it. Can

you come to the meeting today after school? Ms. Wyman's room?"

"I'll be there," says DuShawn. I notice he's avoiding looking at Tonni, on account of her being about ready to commit murder with her eyeballs and all.

Addie and I start to walk away when we notice how quiet the cafeteria has gotten. It's like the room itself is holding its breath. Addie steps into the moment.

Sweeping her left arm dramatically in DuShawn's direction, she lets out with, "DuShawn Carter—the Freedom Party's candidate for president of the student council!"

The place erupts in cheers.

Addie never ceases to amaze me.

9

BY THE time I get to art class, which is last period of the day, I am the Freedom Party candidate for treasurer. I do not know how this happened. I suspect it went something like this:

Addie: So, Bobby, you'll be treasurer, okay?

Me: Okay.

If you are wondering why it never occurs to me to say no to Addie, that is because you do not know Addie. Or me. Addie does not take no for an answer, and I do not know how to give it for one.

Another thing I have said yes to is asking Colin Briggs if he will run for secretary. I think Colin running for secretary makes even less sense than me running for treasurer, and I tell Addie so.

Me: Colin is a boy. He will not want to run for secretary.

Addie: You are a sexist pig. Colin won't care. Besides, he likes to write.

Me: But shouldn't we have another girl on the ticket?

(I ask this, thinking surely this will make sense to Addie, who is such a feminist she once wrote a letter to her church asking that "hymns" be called "hers." She did not succeed.)

Addie: You have a point, but let's ask Colin first. As much as I hate admitting it, I think it's important that we have one other popular person on the ballot.

I find this logic distinctly un-Addie-like, considering that there are popular *girls* we could ask, but I do not at that moment possess the crucial nugget of information that will later explain her odd behavior.

What I do know is this: While Colin is one of the popular kids, he is different from most of them. He is nice, for one thing. Not that some of the other popular kids aren't nice, but they have different ways of showing it, depending on who's on the receiving end. When Brittney talks to you, for instance, you get the feeling she is being polite and showing that she knows how to behave around those less fortunate than herself. Sort of like she's Mother Teresa and you're a leper.

Colin isn't like that. He acts the same with everybody, so that you end up feeling like an actual person around him.

He is also one of those people who are good at everything they do, but you do not hate him for this, because it does not swell his head to the size of a watermelon. For example, he is a natural athlete, but doesn't go around talking sports all the time or thinking it is the end of the world if his team doesn't win. In fact, he is quiet for a boy, and does not favor rude words or sounds such as those produced by sticking your hand in your armpit and giving it a squeeze.

When I walk into Mr. Minelli's room, I am a few minutes late, on account of Mrs. DePaolo having stopped me in the hall and asking if I could help her pick up about a thousand flyers she had just dropped on the floor.

I hand my late pass to Mr. Minelli, then sit down in my seat across from Joe and get ready to dirty my hands with charcoal. Joe's going at his drawing so hard he doesn't even notice me come in, although I am suspecting the real reason he doesn't look up has more to do with one of the two characters sitting on either side of him than his passion for drawing.

One of these characters is Kelsey Scoggins. She's the new girl I told you about who is so shy you can hardly notice her breathing. Mr. Minelli is always looking over her shoulder and making *mm-hmm* noises because, like I say, he thinks Kelsey is a genius. Whenever he holds up her work to show the rest of the class, which he's already done about three times and we've only had four classes, Kelsey puts her head down on her desk and dies. I'm guessing though that her talent as an artist is what keeps her going. I mean, shyness that bad isn't just part of your personality, it's like an illness, and I'll bet on a stack of waffles that it hurts like one.

You probably thought I was going to say pancakes there, didn't you?

Well, anyhow, whilst I'm sitting there staring at her, without realizing that's what I'm doing, she looks up and makes eye contact with me for about a nanosecond and that's enough to turn her cheeks the color of a strawberry shake and get her ducking her head back down so that her hair falls in front of her eyes, but not before I make out what I'm almost positive is a smile.

Then I'm thinking, *I never noticed that Kelsey Scoggins is pretty.* This thought does not surprise me too much because, after all, hardly anybody notices Kelsey. But the following thought *does* surprise me, and it is this: *I think maybe she likes me.*

Then I think, *Yeah, right. A pretty girl, even one who is socially handicapped like Kelsey Scoggins, does not like a boy like me.*

And what is a boy like me? you may ask.

Even if you did not, I will tell you: A boy like me is fat.

There, I said it.

I am relieved to be pulled away from these thoughts by the sound of the person on the other side of Joe. He is all of a sudden talking to Joe in a low voice, pointing at Joe's drawing, and Joe is saying things back like, "Really? You really think it's good?"

Joe is acting like a Joe when he says these things, not a JoDan or a Scorpio, and it is funny at first to see him acting this way, almost what I would call normal, but then I think it isn't all that funny because the person he is talking to is Colin.

After class, I go over to Colin, who is at the sink washing charcoal off his hands. I am only slightly nervous about approaching him because, like I say, he is not too hard to talk to, and so I need only a handful of fake conversation-starters before getting down to business.

"Addie and I were wondering—well, you heard about the Freedom Party, right?—well, we were wondering if you would like to be on our ticket."

I do not let on yet that we're talking about secretary here.

"Oh, gee, I'm really sorry, Bobby," he says, like he honestly means it, "but I'm already running on another ticket."

"For secretary?" I ask. I cannot seem to keep this to myself.

Colin smiles. "No, vice president."

"With Brittney?"

He shakes his head. "Drew," he says. "I'm a Democrat."

"Oh," I say. I have run out of dialogue. Sometimes I wish I were a character in a book and there was a writer out there giving me things to say. This is one of those times. I just stand there, feeling stupid.

"It's too bad I didn't know before the nominating convention," Colin says, wiping his hands on a paper towel and making way for me at the sink. "I mean, I don't know if I would have said yes or not. Drew's my friend and all, but . . . well, I think Addie's really smart. I have a lot of respect for her. Good luck," he says and walks away.

I turn and see that he slows down when he passes Joe and Kelsey, who are standing a few people behind me in line, talking to each other. I watch carefully to make out if Kelsey's lips are actually moving, but it is mostly Joe doing the talking, and I notice his lips speed up just when Colin slows down.

Fifteen minutes later—if you believe the clock in the hall, and twenty-one minutes later if you believe the clock in Ms. Wyman's room—I tell Addie Colin said no. Her face practically falls off she is so disappointed, but then she pulls it right back on.

"No sense dwelling on it," she says. Addie, as you

have no doubt surmised by now, is a mover and a shaker. She rarely dwells.

So we are huddled at the back of Ms. Wyman's room—Addie, DuShawn, and me—when Addie goes, "Okay, we have to plan our strategy quickly. The Democrats and Republicans held their conventions during seventh period and they've put together their slates and their platforms. We're still short a candidate and we don't have our platform."

"I thought it was 'Free the Slaves,'" DuShawn quips and Addie gives him a look that needs no interpretation. "Anyway," he goes on, returning the look, "what makes you think Ms. Wyman is going to allow the Freedom Party to exist?"

"Simple—because she has to." Addie raises her voice to accommodate the growing din of middle-school politicians filling the room. "I went to the office after lunch and asked to see the student council bylaws." She pulls out a piece of paper on which she's written, "More than two parties shall be allowed if the additional parties can prove they serve a purpose not served by the existing parties."

"I'm tellin' you—'Free the Slaves,'" DuShawn says

again. "No way the other two parties are gonna have *that* as their platform."

"Is it genetic coding or something that boys can't be serious?" Addie goes.

DuShawn rolls his eyes. I get the feeling he's as serious about this whole political party thing as I am. Which is to say: not. I know that I'm involved because Addie is my friend and I don't know how to say no. I have not yet figured DuShawn's angle.

All of a sudden, Addie gets all excited. "Look around the room," she says. "What do you see? More to the point, what *don't* you see?"

We look around the room.

"I do not see any fish," DuShawn gives.

"And," I put in, "I note a discernible absence of lawn ornaments."

DuShawn cracks up and flashes his palm for a high five, which I give him—or almost, anyway; I'm off-center so it's more like a high three—and I'm well on my way to totally betraying my lifelong friendship with Addie for the buzz I'm feeling from having actually made a certifiable popular person laugh *with* me and not *at* me when Ms. Wyman marches into the room with so much authority I pop up out of my seat ready to sing "God Save the Queen."

"Yes, Mr. Goodspeed?" Ms. Wyman asks, noting that I am the only one standing.

"May I be excused?" I ask. I cannot think what else to say.

Addie looks at me as if I have completely lost my mind, which I venture to say I have. When Ms. Wyman gives me permission to leave, I shrug at Addie and mouth, "I'll be right back." She mouths back, "You are made of gorgonzola."

That probably isn't what she says, but that's what it looks like.

Anyway, while counting to a hundred outside Ms. Wyman's room, I suddenly spot Skeezie Tookis lurking down the hall. I would like to think there is another word to describe his behavior, but "lurking" is a perfect fit. Ordinarily, Skeezie is not a lurker. Even those of an adult persuasion who have called him a young hooligan have never combined the accusation with the word "lurk" or any of its derivatives. Yet, there he is. Lurking.

"Skeeze!" I call out in a hushed sort of way, not wanting Ms. Wyman to hear me and suddenly appear in the hall to ask why I needed to be excused in order to count to a hundred.

The Skeeze looks over his shoulder, but not like he has heard me and not so far that he sees me. He's got this whole furtive way about him, which makes sense, considering that he is lurking and all. I wonder what he is up to, but I do not call out to him again. Instead, I pull myself back behind a fire extinguisher, so that if he happens to look down the hall in my direction he will not see me. Although he *will* see a fire extinguisher with legs. I pop my head out just in time to catch him in the act of shoving something through the slots of a locker. I make out which locker it is and wait for Skeezie to cease his lurking and scurry away. Actually, he does not scurry. He cops an attitude and moves down the hall bobbing his head and snapping his fingers, like he's John Travolta in that movie *Grease*. It's a relief seeing him act like himself, and the thought occurs to me that in the space of a couple of hours all my friends have been acting strange. The theme to *Invasion of the Body Snatchers* starts playing inside my head. I have *got* to stop watching all these old movies.

Why in the world, I am thinking, *would Skeezie be putting something in Colin Briggs's locker?*

"Ninety-eight, ninety-nine, one hundred," I say. I turn around and bump smack into Addie.

"Is your mental health break over?" she asks. "Because if it is, you are desperately needed inside. Ms. Wyman is threatening to disallow the Freedom Party. You've got to help us convince her that we serve a purpose not served by the other parties."

"*Do* we have a purpose?" I ask.

"Of course," Addie says. "DuShawn and I worked it all out. We are the party who speaks on behalf of the minority students of Paintbrush Falls Middle School."

"Who am *I* supposed to speak on behalf of?" I give back. "The overweight and undervocal?"

Addie does not find this funny or even seem to hear me. She is staring at something past my right shoulder. I turn and look but nothing is there.

"Let's go," she says. And we do.

87

10

DuShawn: What are you doing?

Addie: Writing down what you say.

DuShawn: That is so gay.

Addie: Excuse me?

DuShawn: That's so gay, y'know, weird.

Addie: I <u>hate</u> that expression. Gay does <u>not</u> equal weird.

DuShawn: Whatever. So why are you writing everything down?

Addie: Because that's what we do when we have a Forum.

DuShawn: Say what?

Addie: I told you. Skeezie, Joe, Bobby, and I get together and talk about important issues.

Bobby: Over ice cream.

Addie: Over ice cream.

Skeezie: Or sodas.

Addie: The point is we talk about important issues and we call it the Forum. These are the minutes.

Bobby: <u>You</u> should run for secretary.

Addie: No, thanks. Oh, but stroke of genius. I'm going to ask Heather O'Malley if she'll run.

JoDan: Heather O'Malley?

DuShawn: She's Chinese.

Addie: And adopted. Two minorities in one.

Bobby: I can't believe Ms. Wyman agreed to let the Freedom Party run on the basis of representing minorities.

Addie: That was my whole point when I said look around the room. DuShawn was the <u>only</u> member of a minority group there.

JoDan: Excuse me. He was the only <u>visible</u> member of a minority group. There are all kinds of minorities.

Skeezie: Yeah, you said it yourself a minute ago. Heather's adopted. You wouldn't know that from looking at her.

89

DuShawn: Uh, did you ever meet the rest of her family? She's got a mother and father, two sisters, and one brother and they all got freckles and curly red hair. And there she is with her straight black hair and slanty eyes and they name her Heather! Man, the least they coulda done was name her Ming-Li or Kim or somethin'. Sometimes, people got no sense.

Addie: Why should they give her a Chinese name? Why does that make a difference?

DuShawn: Give her a sense of pride, man! The girl's Chinese. Callin' her Heather and stickin' her in the middle of a family of micks, man, just makes her look the fool.

Skeezie: Whoa. What'd you just say?

DuShawn: What part?

Skeezie: The part about micks. My mom's half-Irish, man.

DuShawn: Oh, man, I didn't mean nothin' by it. It's just a name.

Skeezie: Yeah, so are other words I could think of.

They're just names, too. I don't know what
<u>you</u> think about them, but I know what
your friend Tonni would say.

DuShawn: Man, don't be quotin' Tonni at me, okay?
She's always ready for a fight, acting like
we're some kind of oppressed people just
because we're black. But, hey, as far's I can
tell, you people got it worse than us.

Addie: Who are "you people"?

DuShawn: You guys. The Gang of Five or whatever you
call yourselves. You're more oppressed than
Tonni and Royal and me. I mean, we're cool.
You guys are the ones who have to watch
your butts all the time.

Addie: Thanks a lot.

DuShawn: I'm just tellin' it like I see it. No offense
meant.

Skeezie: So does being cool mean you get to go around
calling other people names?

Bobby: Skeezie . . .

DuShawn: It's all right. I shouldn't have said micks,
okay?

Addie: Or talked about Heather having slanty eyes.

DuShawn: Now what's up with that? You afraid of saying slanty eyes if the girl's got slanty eyes? What color skin I got?

Addie: Black.

DuShawn: That is right. I got skin the color of night, and I'm proud of it. There's no reason to look away, act like it's somethin' other than it is. Girl's got slanty eyes, she's got slanty eyes. Tonni's got black skin, too, and kinkiest hair you ever did see.

JoDan: Her hair is <u>fabulous</u>.

DuShawn: And Royal's got skin the color of mocha latte, man. And you . . .

Addie: Me?

DuShawn: Yeah, you. You got skin the color of I don't know what, the inside of almonds. How come you stop writin'?

Addie: No reason.

DuShawn: Well, you get my point. The color of your skin or the shape of your eyes doesn't matter.

Addie: It <u>shouldn't</u> matter, but it does. And that's

           <u>my</u> point. I was reading in <u>The New York</u>

           <u>Times</u> about this study—

Skeezie: Our ice cream's probably sitting over there on

           the counter, melting. Who's working today?

           Oh, it's that new one. HellomynameisSteffi.

           I'll cut her some slack. She's a babe.

Addie: As in the pig of book and movie fame?

Skeezie: As in hot. Ow!

Addie: <u>You're</u> the pig. Anyway, this study in the

           <u>Times</u> showed that state police are more

           likely to pull drivers over to the side of the

           road if they have dark skin. I mean, that is

           <u>so</u> wrong.

Bobby: There you go again, Addie, quoting from <u>The</u>

           <u>New York Times</u>. You can't go throwing that

           stuff around when you're running for office

           here. What exactly is the Freedom Party

           going to do for minority students <u>here</u>?

Addie: We're going to make sure that their voices

           are heard and that the school administration

           is sensitive to their needs. Anyway, I don't

	have all the answers. That's why DuShawn

have all the answers. That's why DuShawn
is on the ticket—and hopefully Heather, too.
That way we can hear from <u>them</u> what they
need.

Skeezie: So, DuShawn, my man, what do you need?

DuShawn: I need my hot-fudge sundae, man, and I
need it <u>now</u>!

Skeezie: Right on!

Addie: Skeezie, if you do not stop snapping your
fingers . . .

DuShawn: I'm thinkin'. Maybe it's more the color of
peach ice cream.

Addie: Huh?

DuShawn: Your skin, girl. I'm talkin' about your skin.

11

SO HERE I am at the Candy Kitchen, in the back booth with the torn red leatherette upholstery, squeezed in a little tighter than usual on account of DuShawn being added into the picture, and while the others are exercising their jaws, with me throwing in my own two cents from time to time, I am blissfully unaware that the events that will unfold in the days to follow will change the course of my life. I mean, how *could* I know that? How could anybody?

When you're living through them, events are nothing more than stuff that happens. You're not thinking about significance. Significance only comes when you look back at your life. At the moment, what you're thinking is whether you've got enough money in your pocket for hot fudge or you should just order a single scoop. And when one of your best friends is all hopped up about an election you don't care a Fig Newton about, what's agitating *your* brain is whether you should ask this cute, artistic, and terminally shy girl who kind of smiled at you one time for a nano-second (you think) (maybe) if she wants to come over to your friend Joe's house on Sunday night to help make posters. And before you can work up the nerve to ask her, you will catch yourself sniffing your armpits, slap-ping yourself on the forehead like your head and your hand are two of the Three Stooges, and calling your-self an incurable geek.

I take no pride in mentioning these things. Would that I could say I am caught up in Addie's passion for social justice and the electoral process. Would that I could tell you, "Sniff my own armpits? Never!" But if I am going to all the bother of writing stuff down, it may as well be the truth. And the truth is that I am not a particularly high-minded character in my formative years. I hardly ever speak up in class and I never ques-tion what the teacher says. I am just a get-along kind of guy. Like my dad. I am certain I will be the face in the yearbook everybody will look at and say, "Bobby Goodspeed? I don't remember anybody named Bobby Goodspeed."

But of course it will not turn out this way. The future is a trickster rabbit, full of surprises. Only the past is predictable.

Somehow, I *do* work up the nerve on Friday to ask Kelsey if she wants to help out with the posters. This of course is after the aforementioned armpit-sniffing episode, which fortunately goes unwitnessed. Kelsey says yes—or, at least, I think she does. She talks so softly I can't be entirely sure, but she does take the piece of paper I give her with Joe's address on it and gives back one of those blink-and-you'll-miss-it smiles of hers.

We decide to make the posters at Joe's house because Pam, being a painter and all, has offered to help out and has lots of art supplies she is willing to donate to the cause. From my personal point of view, this is more than copacetic, although I try not to dwell on the prospect of being with Pam and Kelsey in the same room at the same time for fear of becoming light-headed and making a large noise when my oxygen-deprived body hits the ground.

On Friday aṫ Awkworth & Ames, my mind is occupied with these thoughts, having nothing better to do, when Mr. Kellerman spooks me by coming up out of nowhere and saying, "Mr. Goodspeed, do you know the first thing about selling ties?"

I own as I do not, although I stake a claim on a pretty decent fashion sense, on account of my long-standing friendship with a certain party by the name of Joe Bunch.

Mr. Kellerman does not get this, but he does not question it. All he goes is, "Let's put that fashion sense to the test, shall we?" He is holding a stack of dress shirts, some with stripes, some with checks, and some that are solid colors. I get the sense that he has finally figured out a way to keep himself entertained and I am it.

For the next twenty minutes, he dares me to pick out ties to go with these shirts and I take up the challenge. To tell you the truth, I am having a good time of it, except for those occasions when the Killer Man clicks his tongue and informs me, with a kind of pleasure I can only describe as oily, that I have committed a fashion faux pas, which is French for "screw-up." Even when I make what is obviously a cool match, the highest praise he will give is, "Not bad." Or, "For one so young, you have a decent intuitive sense." Do not count on getting an "awesome" or a high five out of Mr. Kellerman.

Still, I can tell that he is surprised I am so good at this and is wishing he could come up with a harder test for me, something I would be sure to fail, because that is what he really wants: for me to fail so he can lord it over me. That is the entertainment part of the program. But even when he is being nice to me, he's nasty about it, and I am beginning to feel fed up and wishing I were more like Skeezie or Addie so I could tell him what he can do with his ties.

"Not that!" he snaps impatiently at one point, just because I have the nerve to select a tie with a cartoon character on it. He slaps my hand and makes a face like I have drawn nose hairs on the *Mona Lisa* or something.

"Ouch," I say, even though the slap hurts my ego more than my wrist.

"Well, I'm sorry, but ties like that go with *nothing*. Do you hear me, Mr. Goodspeed, *nothing*."

I nod, knowing there is no point in trying to convince him of my own personal belief that Daffy Duck goes with *everything*. Do you hear me, Mr. Kellerman, *everything*.

Just then, a customer shows. Before we both faint dead away, Mr. K says to me, "Now watch and perhaps you can learn a thing or two."

The woman he approaches is young and unsure of herself. She looks like she took a wrong turn and is wondering how she ended up in this mausoleum and if she will ever see her loved ones again.

"May I help you?" Mr. Kellerman oozes. He pulls his lips back into a virtual smile. The effect is creepy.

"Um, I guess," goes the woman. She is maybe twice my age. "I need a gift."

"Of course." Without asking who the gift is for, Mr. Kellerman starts showing her ties that make the woman's eyes glaze over.

When she holds up a yellow tie with bright red zig-zags running through it and asks, "What about this one?" Mr. Kellerman looks like she has just thrust a plate of leeches at him and said, "Care for an appetizer?"

"Ah, wellll . . ." he goes, when he is called away to the phone.

I don't know which of them is more relieved, but I can see the woman is eyeing the exit and I figure it's now or never, so I step in and say, "That tie definitely makes a statement. If you like it, perhaps I can show you some others along the same lines."

Five minutes later, I am ringing up a sale for *four* ties and the woman is thanking me for all my help. I cannot wait for Mr. Kellerman to get off the phone so I can brag shamelessly, but when he does get off the phone I do not brag shamelessly or in any other adverbial manner, because he doesn't look in my direction or ask what happened with the customer or even notice that Daffy is missing.

His face is getting that melting cheese look again, and I am wondering what gives when he says,

"I must . . ." and leaves the words lying there, flat and useless as a couple of pieces of fallen baloney with no dog around to lap them up.

He goes off and I'm left standing there, feeling good about the sale I've just made but with nobody to brag to, while at the same time trying to figure what's up with Mr. K, all to the accompaniment of Mickey and the Accordionaires doing their nursing-home rendition of "Y.M.C.A." (I do not believe there is such a group as Mickey and the Accordionaires. Out of sheer boredom I have come up with names for the musicians I imagine performing each of the Muzak melodies I am forced to listen to every time I work at Awkworth & Ames. I call the *oo-ah* chorus that performs "Raindrops Keep Falling on My Head" the Vowelettes.)

The Killer Man does not return. When Junior Fernell shows up to fill in for him, he tells me only that Mr. K was called away on personal business. I do not press Junior Fernell, because I do not really like him. Besides, I can tell right away that he needs to feel important and that divulging too much information to an underling would seriously threaten his status as Son of the Store Manager and Heir Apparent to the Realm.

While Junior busies himself refolding clothing that is more in need of dusting than refolding, and tidying up the sales desk, which Mr. Kellerman has already tidied to the point where it could pass military inspection, I alternately replay my coup as a tie salesman and imagine what sort of personal business took Mr. K away. I want to think he is involved in some type of illegal drug operation that is about to be exposed, bringing national attention to Paintbrush Falls. I picture myself watching myself on TV going, "Yeah, I worked with Mr. Kellerman. No, he never struck me as the criminal type. I was as surprised as anybody to find out he was a drug czar and that he had fourteen bodies buried in his backyard. I mean, people at work *did* call him Killer Man, it's true, but who would have thought..."

This is when the Muzak stops and the voice says, "Shoppers, the store will be closing in fifteen minutes."

"Kind of a slow day," Junior Fernell goes, like there's any other kind at Awkworth & Ames. "Why don't you cut out early? I can close up."

I say thanks, knowing that Junior is doing this not out of kindness but so he can feel like a big shot, but I am truly grateful, anyway, because if I stick around much longer my sanity is in serious danger.

12

BY THE time Sunday evening rolls around, I am no longer thinking about Mr. Kellerman. Truth be told, by the time I am out the door of Awkworth & Ames on Friday, I am no longer thinking about Mr. Kellerman. I am too caught up in my own mixed-up life to worry about his. Although I do have a moment watching the news with my dad Friday night when I swear the anchor guy says to the anchor woman, "Well, Jenny, pretty shocking news from Upstate New York today. Seems a clothing salesman in the little town of Paintbrush Falls has been revealed to be a Mafia godfather." Of course, what he actually is saying turns out to have nothing to do with Upstate New York or a small-town clothing salesman or even organized crime, which just shows what an overworked imagination combined with a pathetic need for excitement does to the brain.

Anyway, by Sunday evening what I *am* thinking about is Kelsey Scoggins. I go so far as to call Skeezie on Saturday and ask him what he knows about love.

"Not you, too!" he gives back, although when I prod him for an explanation, he zips his lips and goes, "All I know about love is that it's a four-letter word."

"Why so cynical?" I ask.

Skeezie gives his bubble gum a pop on the other end. "Oh, gee, I don't know. Could it have something to do with my dad splittin' two years ago and my mom still cursing him out every chance she gets and my little sisters still cryin' themselves to sleep at night? Hm, let me think about it. Time's up. Yep, that's it."

Me: Lots of people get divorced, Skeezie.

Skeezie: And your point is?

Me: My point is it doesn't *have* to turn you into a cynic.

Skeezie: Says you. Why's it on everybody's brain all of a sudden, anyways?

Me: We're in seventh grade. Our hormones are kicking in.

Skeezie: So who's kickin' your hormones in, Bobsters? As if I didn't know.

Me: Who told you?

Skeezie: I got eyes, man.

Me: You're not even *in* my art class. You've never even *seen* me talking to Kelsey.

Skeezie: Kelsey? I thought you were talkin' about Joe's aunt Pam.

The sound Skeezie doesn't hear is me blushing.

Me: I guess it's kind of both.

Skeezie: In the words of Joe Bunch—*oy*.

On Sunday night, it's Skeezie and me, DuShawn and Joe and Kelsey, and the magnolia-scented Pam, down in Joe's basement with poster board and markers everywhere. One whiff of Pam and I'm praying for ventilation.

Joe's parents are home, along with his brother Jeff, but they're not in the way. Jeff is up in his room on his computer, which is pretty much where he lives, and Joe's parents come in and out only every so often to make sure we're taken care of in the refreshments department.

"Don't want to have any starving artists," Joe's father cracks at one point, and we all laugh up a storm like it's Dad Appreciation Month.

Joe has cool parents, there are no two ways about it. Joe says it is impossible to hate them, at a time in life when hating your parents starts feeling like a requirement. When Pam split up with her boyfriend a few years back and was feeling all messed up and sorry for herself, she called her sister, who is Joe's mom, and was told, "Get on the next train out of New York and come stay with us for as long as you need." It's been two years now and Pam has said more than once that Joe's mom and dad saved her life.

Joe says the same thing about Pam. He calls her his fairy godmother, because she showed up just at the moment in his life when he needed somebody to let him know it was okay to be himself. Pam always tells him, "You didn't need me. You had your parents. You would have been just fine."

I agree with Pam, but Joe doesn't buy it. He insists that if his aunt hadn't come along when she did, by now he would be calling other guys "dude" and pretending to like football and hating himself inside. I say that's just Joe being dramatic, but I never say it to him.

Meanwhile, Addie is going on and on about the Freedom Party and how we have to have posters that really stand out and how we need a symbol because the Republicans have the elephant and the Democrats have the donkey.

It turns out that Heather O'Malley said no to being on the Freedom Party ticket. After getting turned down by every other minority student she could think of— except Tonni, who she didn't ask—Addie begged Skeezie, and Skeezie, to her surprise, said yes.

"Man, it was pitiful," Skeezie tells me. "The girl was desperate, what could I do? Besides, there is not a chance we are going to win, so it's not like I have to worry about actually *doing* anything. Although there is the factor of public humiliation up until the elections, but, hey, I'm used to that."

Not the best reason to run for office, but I am willing to bet there have been worse.

Anyway, when I see Skeezie and Addie with their

heads together at one point during the evening, I find it kind of strange but assume it has to do with the campaign. I am wrong, as I will find out later.

The way it goes with posters is this: Addie and DuShawn are working together. Joe and Kelsey are working together. And Pam and I are working together. Which explains why for a period of time previously considered humanly impossible, I maintain my life force without benefit of breathing. I am actually relieved not to be working with Kelsey, because then I would have to deal with not breathing *and* coming up with something to say. Kelsey is the quietest person I have ever met. With Joe, it doesn't matter; he does all the talking. Pam is also chatting away while we work (I figure it must run in the family), telling me all about these paintings she's just finished and how this friend of hers is trying to get her a job at a gallery in New York City and, as if transitions had never been invented, how great it is that we are all doing this, meaning the Freedom Party, and I just keep going *uh-huh* to everything she says and clamping my arms to my sides so I don't drip sweat on fresh marker.

You may have noticed that I have not mentioned what the Skeeze is doing. That is because he is not working on the posters. He has taken it upon himself as secretary of the Freedom Party to lie around on the sofa reading *People* magazine.

Before we can start on the posters, however, we have to choose a symbol and a slogan. These are the ones we vote on:

Freedom for One, Freedom for All (dolphin)—Kelsey
Freedom Rocks! (guitar)—Skeezie
Be Strong, Be Cool, Let Freedom Rule! (Madonna)—Joe
Fly Like a Bird, Let Freedom Be Heard (dove)—Addie

DuShawn and I do not make any suggestions, except for DuShawn's "Down with Slavery!" (watermelon), which nobody takes seriously, including DuShawn. I am learning he has a wicked sense of humor and think this is an admirable trait. Joe and Skeezie agree, but Addie is not so sure and her lips get a little puckery when she talks about it.

Anyway, Kelsey's idea wins and we spend the next

hour copying pictures of dolphins out of wildlife maga-
zines and writing:

> Freedom for One, Freedom for All!
> Vote for the **FREEDOM PARTY**
> And <u>your</u> voice <u>will</u> be heard!
> Our candidates <u>care</u>!
> President . . . DuShawn Carter
> Vice President . . . Addie Carle
> Treasurer . . . Bobby Goodspeed
> Secretary . . . Skeezie Tookis
> Isn't it time for a <u>change</u>?

We are all congratulating ourselves on how brilliant we are and how Brittney and the Republicans
and Drew and the Democrats don't stand a chance
against us (not that any of us except Addie believes
this, but it is easy to get caught up in campaign fever),
when Joe's mom comes in and tells Addie her mom
has just called and she needs to get home. I personally am glad, because I do not think I can stand being
so near to Pam any longer, what with her giving off the
scent of magnolias the way she does.

Being so up close and personal with Pam, I have forgotten to think about Kelsey for whole minutes at a time and now I notice out of the corner of my occuli that Joe is still chatting up a regular storm with her and she is listening with both her ears and laughing in a quiet but semihysterical sort of way, and when her dad arrives and she's saying her goodbyes, she gives Joe the same now-you-see-it-now-you-don't smile she gave me just last week. And this gets me to wondering, but I am not entirely sure what it is I am wondering about.

DuShawn leaves when Addie does, but the Skeeze and I do not have to depart immediately, so we retire with Joe to his room, where he invites us to hang out.

"Hey, Joey," Skeezie says as he turns on Joe's Lava lamp and we settle in on the lime green shag carpet. "Looks like Kelsey's got quite the thing for you, my man. She was on you like fleas on a dog."

"What?" says Joe.

"Not that you weren't encouraging it. You kept talkin' and talkin' and she kept listenin' and listenin' and laughin' at your dumb jokes."

"So?"

"So she likes you."

"So?"

"Just makin' an observation." Skeezie turns to me. "Sorry, Bobby, 'cause I know you've got this major crush on her and all."

My cheeks turn the color of the big red glob rising to the top of Joe's Lava lamp. Do I have a crush on Kelsey? I think maybe I do, but then being around Pam tonight I'm not so sure. I decide that I hate hormones.

Joe shrugs. "I'm just being nice to her," he says. "Nobody talks to her because she doesn't talk back. And my jokes are *not* dumb, for your information. I happen to be a very funny person. Anyway, if Bobby likes Kelsey, he can have her."

"Nice," I go. "Like she's a cookie that fell on the floor."

"I don't mean it that way," says Joe. He starts picking at the carpet while Skeezie finds a Koosh ball to toss around.

"Well, what *do* you mean?" Skeezie asks, bouncing the Koosh ball off his knee.

"I mean if Bobby likes Kelsey, he can have her. Hello."

"I thought you'd be happy she likes you. I thought havin' a girl like you was supposed to be the key to eternal happiness or somethin'."

"Boy," I say, "for somebody who thinks love is a four-letter word, you sure do have it on the brain a lot."

"Just makin' conversation," says the Skeeze.

"Well, here's a three-letter word to help the conversation along, okay?" Joe says. He stops his picking, which gets Skeezie to stop his bouncing, and they eyeball each other. "G-a-y."

"Huh?"

"I've told you before, Skeezie. I'm gay."

"You said you thought *maybe* you were. I didn't exactly believe you."

"Well, now I'm telling you I am."

"You don't *know* that."

"Don't tell me what I don't know. Look around my room, okay? What do you see?"

Skeezie gives Joe's room the once-over and starts ticking off what he eyes: books, CDs, computer, tie-dyed butterfly chair with smiley face pillow, big stuffed flamingo on the bed, antique floor lamp with fringed shade, posters of Madonna and Cher and Leonardo DiCaprio in a T-shirt.

"So?" he says when he's done taking inventory. "So you're a little weird. We all are. That's why we're friends."

"There are different shades of weird, Skeezie. Mine's pink."

"Look," Skeezie says, " I know you're kind of girly— no offense—but that doesn't mean you have to like boys."

"True," says Joe.

"So how do you know you do?" Skeezie asks.

"How do you know you like girls?" Joe throws back at him.

Skeezie laughs. "I *don't* like girls. I mean, I don't like girls right now. But I like *lookin'* at them and all. And I guess maybe one day . . . geez, I don't know how I know, Joe, I just do. I don't have to think about it."

"Well," says Joe, "that's how it is with me and boys. I don't have to think about it."

This stops Skeezie cold and he resumes his Koosh ball tossing. I can tell he's thinking by the way his face is all scrunched up.

Finally, he says, "What do your mom and dad say about it?"

Joe shrugs. "I've never come right out and told them I'm gay, but I think they know. I mean, they're not stupid. No offense."

"None taken," Skeezie says.

"They've always let me just be myself, you know? Playing with dolls and dressing up and all that, they never told me it was wrong. Of course, they never told me it was right, either. So I worried a lot, especially about my dad. I figured he probably wanted a son who was a lot more like Jeff. It was Pam who helped me see that Mom and Dad were letting me be who I was instead of trying to make me into something else. She told me that was just about the best kind of love anybody could give anybody."

Skeezie nods. "Your parents are all right," he says. "Still, it's got to be tough. Being gay and all."

"Why do you think that?"

"Well, take the dance, for instance. If Bobby wants to go to the dance with Kelsey—"

I start to object.

"I'm just sayin'," Skeezie says, heading me off. "If

Bobby wants to, and let's just say for the sake of argument that Kelsey wants to go with him, well, that's okay. Nobody's gonna make a big deal of it, y'know? But what if *you* want to go with somebody?"

"I do," says Joe, before he thinks to stop himself. He glances my way on account of my knowing his secret.

"You do?" says Skeezie. "Who?"

"Not that it's going to happen," Joe says. "But I like . . . somebody."

"Come on, give."

"You won't tell anybody?"

"Jo*Dan*. It's *me*. The Skeeze."

"Okay, okay. I like Colin, all right?"

"Colin?"

"Yes, but if you tell anybody . . . I would've told you before this, Skeezie, but I don't know . . . I wasn't sure you'd understand."

"Oh, man," Skeezie says, hitting the side of his head with his hand. "Did you know about this, Bobby?"

"Uh-huh," I say. "Since the end of fifth grade."

"Why didn't you tell me? If I'd known last week, even, it would've saved me . . . oh, I feel so stupid, man. What's Addie gonna say?"

"Addie? What's she got to do with anything?"

Skeezie leans in, like he's going to tell us some big secret, which in fact he is. "You gotta promise not to tell her I told you, okay?"

"Pinky swear," Joe goes, and Skeezie gives him a look.

"Addie likes Colin, too, man, and I told her I'd be, like, a go-between."

"So *that's* why you were putting something in Colin's locker!" I say. "I saw you."

Joe asks, "What did you see?"

"I'll bet it was a 'somebody-likes-you' note. Am I right?"

Skeezie nods. "I'm trying to fix them up."

"So much for being a cynic about love," I go.

"I am for *me*," Skeezie answers. "No reason other people can't be happy. If that's what they want."

Joe gets quiet. "It doesn't matter," he says. "Go ahead and fix Addie up with Colin. She's got a lot better chance than I do. Who am I kidding?"

All of a sudden, we're both staring at Joe—Skeezie and me—like we've never seen him before. I'm thinking about the first time I ever laid eyes on him, him standing there behind the screen door wearing a dress and all, telling me he's a boy, and I get to wondering if Skeezie's remembering the way he used to pick on Joe in kindergarten. Next thing I know, I've got in my head the Easy-Bake Oven Joe got for his birthday when he was six, I think it was, and how much he loved that thing. Whenever I came over to play, he would tell me I had to be the father and he was the mother and he would give me cookies he made himself and I would always say, "You're a good cook, Molly." Because that was his name when he was the mother. Molly.

And then I'm looking over at Skeezie and I am pondering on the fact that his real name is Schuyler and I do not know when he first started getting called Skeezie or dressing like a 1950s young hooligan, but I'm remembering that his dad used to ride around town on a motorcycle, all decked out in a black leather jacket, which is not the usual thing to do in Paintbrush Falls, and he got a lot of grief over it, but he did not care. Or at least that's what he said. But then one day he just up and left.

And then there's me. Pork Chop, Roly-Poly, Fluff.

And I'm thinking there's a lot more to all of us than the names we're called or what we show on the outside.

"Can I tell you guys something?" Joe says. "Will you promise not to laugh at me or say it's gross?"

"Promise," I say, and Skeezie goes, "Pinky swear," and smiles.

"You know what I want more than anything?"

I am guessing by the way he takes a deep breath that the answer to this is not to be found in any of Joe's usual wish-list categories, such as home decor or celebrities-I'd-most-like-to-be-stuck-on-a-desert-island-with.

"I think about this a lot, but I've never told anybody. Not Aunt Pam or anybody. What I want more than anything is to hold hands with somebody I like."

Joe pulls his knees up then, sharp, and crosses his arms over them, so he can lay down his head, like now that he's told us this terrible secret he doesn't want to see our faces telling him what we think.

"Does that gross you out?" he asks from inside his folded-up arms.

"No," I go, and so does the Skeeze.

"If that's how you feel, then you should just go for it, man," says Skeezie, getting all serious. "I mean, you're a pretty outrageous character, JoDan. I never seen you exactly lacking for nerve."

Joe lifts his head.

"Right. Can you see me walking down the hall holding hands with Colin the way Brittney holds hands with Will, or Sara with Justin? Not that I'm saying Colin would *want* to or anything, but it's not fair."

Skeezie nods. "Hey," he goes, "you know what this makes me think of? Remember that time we were in first grade, I think it was, and we went on that field trip over to Saratoga?"

"Uh-huh. You put a worm in my chocolate milk."

"I wasn't thinkin' about that part," goes the Skeeze. "And if it helps any: Sorry about that."

"It helps," says Joe. "So what part were you thinking of?"

"I was thinkin' when we were walkin' down the street that time, remember? After we got off the bus? You had to hold your buddy's hand, and you and I were buddies. Remember?"

Joe nods.

"And this lady goin' by looks at us and she says, 'Aw, aren't you the cutest things?' And after she walks away we look at each other and go, 'Yuck'."

Joe says, "I remember."

"So how come we're not cute anymore? I mean, how come little kids are cute to everybody, doesn't matter what they do, but when you do the same things a little older you aren't cute anymore. Y'know? I mean, what kinda stinkin' deal is that? If you and I were walkin' down the street *now* and we were, y'know, holdin' hands like back when we were buddies in first grade, nobody'd say we were cute. They'd call us fags. Or do somethin' even worse. What's up with *that?*"

We sit there quiet for a time until Joe says, "That's the million-dollar question."

The doorbell rings right below us and I figure it is my dad come to pick up the Skeeze and me.

"Promise you won't tell anybody about Colin," Joe says as we're standing up and Skeezie tosses him the Koosh ball.

We both slap Joe's palm and Skeezie says, "Don't sweat it, buddy."

As I'm riding home and my dad and Skeezie are

shooting the breeze, I get to thinking about the two of them—my dad and the Skeeze—and about Joe, and Addie, too, and Mr. Kellerman and Pam and Kelsey, and even me, and what I'm thinking is this: This business of really knowing people, deep down, including your own self, it is not something you can learn in school or from a book. It takes your whole being to do it—your eyes and your ears, your brain and your heart. Maybe your heart most of all.

I feel like I have figured something out here, something important, something that I thought was hard but turns out to be pretty simple. It doesn't take a genius.

13

THE NEXT morning, Addie and I get to school early so we can put posters up before classes start. I'm standing there with tape on four fingers and Addie is balancing on a folding chair she found someplace when Mrs. DePaolo comes out of the office and says, "Oh, I don't think that's a good idea."

Mrs. DePaolo is the school secretary. She is nice but nervous. Kids are all the time telling her, "It's okay, Mrs. DePaolo." I do not know if this makes her less nervous or more.

"It's okay, Mrs. DePaolo," Addie says. "We're just putting posters up for the election."

Mrs. DePaolo rubs her hands together like she's standing in front of a fire. I think she must have cold blood. She's always got these sweaters draped over her shoulders.

"I know," she says. "I know that's what you're doing. It's just that, oh, did you speak to Mr. Kiley?"

"No. Were we supposed to?"

"Well, I know he wanted to speak with you."

"With us?" Addie asks. "Why? Are we doing something wrong?"

"Oh, my," Mrs. DePaolo says, blowing little puffs of air into her cupped-up hands. I'm definitely right about the cold blood. "I don't think you are, no, of course you're not. It's just that the question was raised, I believe, about . . . oh, I shouldn't get into this, honestly. I think you kids had better talk to Mr. Kiley a.s.a.p., okay? Until then, why don't you hold off putting any posters up?"

A whole bunch of kids pass by. They're looking at us and at the poster Addie is standing there pinning to the wall with her one hand.

"Good luck!" Brittney, a.k.a. Mother Teresa, calls out in a cheery voice.

"Thanks!" Addie the leper calls back.

Kevin Hennessey shouts sarcastically, "Save the whales!" and both Addie and I check out the dolphin on the poster as Mrs. DePaolo shushes Kevin and tells him she hopes she doesn't see him in the office today. The office is Kevin's second home.

Pretty soon, Addie and I are sitting across the desk from Mr. Kiley, who I notice is wearing a flag pin in his lapel. I am wondering if he has always worn this or only since Addie's refusing to say the Pledge, when I further notice that his tie does not go with his shirt. It bothers me. This is the curse of being a tie sales-man. I figure I am doomed to go through the rest of my life noticing whether ties and shirts go together and being bothered if they don't. I think maybe I should quit my job.

Mr. Kiley has been talking and I am tuning in as he says, "I'm sorry, but there's nothing I can do about it."

Addie is perched on the edge of her seat, project-ing her upper body at a sharp angle. She looks like one of those adjustable desk lamps.

"This is so unfair," she is saying. "It's more than unfair. It's not right!"

Mr. Kiley opens his hands wide, palms up, fingers splayed. Adults use this gesture often, especially when talking to kids. They think it means, *Look how honest and open I'm being. Look how hard I've tried. I feel just rotten about it, but I'm absolutely helpless to do anything more than I've already done.* What it really means is, *Conversation's over.*

"But I don't understand," Addie replies to Mr. Kiley's hands. "We met with Ms. Wyman on Thursday. We told her that our party was going to represent the voice of minority students. She didn't tell us then that we couldn't run."

"I repeat: Ms. Wyman spoke to me after school on Friday and made the very good point that both parties state in their platforms that they represent *all* students, which includes minority students. A third party claiming to represent minorities is redundant at the very least and might justifiably be seen as promoting special rights. We don't want that sort of thing here at P.F.M.S., do we?"

"I hardly think that giving minority students a voice is the same as asking for special rights. Besides which, political parties can have the same goals but achieve them through different means. Isn't that true?"

Mr. Kiley nods his head sympathetically. "That's a good point. Look, Addie, I appreciate your passion. I really do. You're a bright girl and you have strong feelings about right and wrong. That's good. But there *is* a system in place and it *works*. Let me encourage you to work within it. If you want to make changes, get involved in the parties that already exist. Talk to the candidates about your concerns and make sure your voice is represented."

"Right," Addie says, "like they'll even listen to us."

"Us?" Mr. Kiley says. "Who do you mean? Other than DuShawn, I don't know who on your ticket *is* a minority, Addie. I'm not sure you know yourself what you're attempting to do here. Between this third-party business and your refusing to say the Pledge, I can't help wondering if what you're *really* after is getting attention. If that's the case, there are better ways to go about it."

Mrs. DePaolo's head is in the door. "Announcements," she says.

Mr. Kiley excuses himself and minutes later Addie and I are walking down the hall with posters tucked under our arms and late passes clutched in our hands, as classroom after classroom pledges its allegiance to the flag of the United States of America and to the republic for which it stands.

We stop at our lockers so we can cram the useless posters in. "I can't believe Kiley accused me of just wanting attention," Addie grouses. "What an insult! I'll bet he never would have said that if I were a boy."

"He was talking to me, too," I point out.

Addie shakes her head. "Mostly he was talking to me. And did you notice what he brought up at the end there? I'll bet this is really about my refusing to say the Pledge. He doesn't like it, and Ms. Wyman just can't stand that I am disobeying one of her little rules. She's all rah-rah self-esteem so long as the self you esteem is the one she approves of. That is *so* hypocritical."

"You're right," I say, "but what can you do? Wyman and Kiley have power and we don't."

"And that's another thing," Addie goes on, slamming her locker door. "Why do adults get to have all the power? Mr. Kiley and Ms. Wyman both say, 'Work within the system.' But it's *their* system! Kids should have power, too. If the student council really *meant* something, we *would* have power!"

"So I guess it's not so bad that the Freedom Party's out of business," I say, "seeing as how the student council doesn't have any real power, anyway."

"Who said we're out of business? We just have to come up with another raison d'être. And when we do, it had better have some teeth in it."

Just then, Kevin Hennessey pops his head out of Ms. Wyman's homeroom, holding a bathroom pass in his hand.

"Yo, Blubber!" he calls out. "You better get a ladder if you're gonna kiss Godzilla!" He laughs as if he actually finds this funny and goes off down the hall, shaking his rear at us.

"He is such an idiot," Addie says, and this gets us both to laughing, which is good because inside I'm still stinging from being called Blubber. It doesn't matter how many times I've been called names, it still hurts—and it still always comes as such a surprise that I never know how to respond. Or maybe I do, but I'm afraid.

As soon as we get inside Ms. Wyman's room we put a lid on our laughter because she's got this look on her face like she has been sharpening her knife and fork and just waiting for our livers to arrive. When we hand her our late passes, she does a quick change into her muffin-baking self, all gooey smiles, but then two seconds later, after Jimmy Lemon pokes me and I tell him to watch it, she makes a personality U-turn and tells me in a tone as tough as stale fruit leather that I'm creating a disturbance and she will not tolerate disturbances in her homeroom.

It is only the third week of school and Ms. Wyman needs a vacation.

In my opinion.

It is on this day that I have my major brainstorm, and when I look back at it, I think it should have occurred to me the minute Kevin Hennessey called out, "Yo, Blubber!" And then I think it should have occurred to me the night before at Joe's house when he and Skeezie and I were sitting around shooting the breeze. Or the time we found that word on Joe's locker. Or the first time I was ever called Fluff. Or one of a thousand other times. In other words, I should have had this major brainstorm a long time ago, but that is not the way life works. Life works like this: You are on the receiving end of all sorts of stuff, but you do not see it clearly. Then all of a sudden you see something happen to somebody else, and the light-bulb goes off over your head.

It happens at lunch.

Addie is filling Skeezie and Joe in on what went on that morning and is so worked up she doesn't even notice the Skeeze swap his box of raisins for her chocolate cake. He starts scarfing it down before she can say anything. I detect this out of the corner of my eye, since I try to avoid watching Skeezie relate to food in an ingestive manner. If his eating habits were a movie, they'd be rated R for violence.

Addie, the anti-Skeeze, spreads a napkin on her lap. "What we have to do is come up with a new platform," she is saying. "Something Ms. Wyman can't dispute. Not that this is really about politics. It's all about Ms. Wyman and her need for control. And revenge."

"Ooo, Cruella De Vil," Joe says, and it is hard to know whether he means this as an insult or a compliment. Cruella is one of Joe's favorite movie characters. Back in second grade he even called himself Cruella. For about a week.

Addie ignores him. "Well, revenge is a paltry weapon when confronted with the arsenal of truth."

Skeezie stares at her with an open mouth, which, given the state it's in, I wish he wouldn't. "Do you make that stuff up on the spot?" he asks Addie. "Or do you stay up nights writing your own material?"

"I can't help it if I have a brilliant mind," Addie says, "and that is *my* cake you just ate."

Skeezie lets out a belch, a loud, lingering, wet one.

Joe turns and looks at him, disgusted. "Couth," he says.

"Thank you," the Skeeze gives back, looking mighty pleased with himself. "Thank you kindly."

I figure all serious conversation has been derailed, and I am right, except that something happens just then that we might not have picked up on if we had been busy knocking our heads together over the new

Freedom Party platform. It is the something that gives me my major brainstorm.

"D-d-d-daryl," I hear. "H-h-how ya d-d-d-doin', D-d-d-daryl?"

"S-s-s-s-stop it, K-k-k-k-k-kevin!"

Kevin Hennessey's laughter is as blunt and heavy as a boot while he watches Daryl Williams slink away from the table his ridicule has forced him to vacate. Gripping the edges of his tray of half-eaten food, Daryl's knuckles turn white and his shoulders hunch up in a desperate attempt to hide the look of humiliation burning his face.

"What a dweeb!" Kevin Hennessey goes, and Jimmy Lemon laughs like Kevin is the funniest guy since Robin Williams.

"That's our raison d'être," I hear myself saying.

The others turn and look at me, and in that split second before I explain, this amazing feeling comes over me. It's a Twilight Zone sort of feeling, like I'm about to pass from one dimension into another. And you know? That's exactly what I'm going to do. I am about to stop being a get-along kind of guy and turn into somebody who makes a difference.

14

"NO MORE names," I say.

Addie goes, "What?"

"That's our platform and that's our party," I explain, getting excited. "The No-Name Party." Ideas are rushing at me like water out of an open hydrant.

The Skeeze, wiping chocolate off his mouth with the back of his hand, says, "What are you talkin' about? The Lame-Brain Party? I don't get it."

"That's because *you're* the lame brain," I tell him. "No offense, Addie, but you've been looking at the wrong minority the whole time. DuShawn even said it."

"Said what?"

Joe chimes in, "He said *we* were the ones who had

to watch our butts, not him and Royal and Tondayala Cherise."

"Right," I go. "And, Joe, you said not every minority is visible, remember? Think about it, Addie, what makes a minority? It's numbers, right? The majority is the larger percentage, the minority the smaller."

"Wyman would be prouda you, man," says the Skeeze, ridding his fingers of unwanted chocolate crumbs by dragging them down the front of his shirt. I swear, his eating is some kind of performance art. He could charge admission.

"Whatever," I say. "The point is that being a minority isn't only about the color of your skin or your religion. It's about not fitting in, being on the outside."

"Like us," Addie goes.

"And Daryl, who Kevin just called a dweeb," I point out. "Think of all the names *we've* been called over the years."

I grab a pen out of my back pocket and start writing down all the names I can think of on a napkin. There are eighteen, then seventeen when I realize I've written "Fluff" twice.

"Wow," Joe says, "that's almost as many as me." He starts rattling off his list and I'm writing so fast the napkin begins to shred. He's got twenty-six by the time he's through and those are only the ones he can think of off the top of his pink-streaked head.

"What about you, Skeeze?" I ask. "What names have you been called?"

Skeezie starts rocking back in his chair, his hands clasped behind his head. "Wop," he starts with, "greaser, greaseball, slimeball, guinea . . ." His list ends up at sixteen, four of which are put-downs of Italians, which doesn't even make sense because Skeezie doesn't have an ounce of Italian blood in him.

It's Addie's turn and now we're all into it, weirdly competing with one another for who's been called the most and the worst names. There are some we've all been called. Addie comes up with only eleven, three of which have to do with her height, five with her brains, and three what we call "all-purpose."

Our final tally covers three napkins. This is what we've got:

BOBBY	JOE	SKEEZIE	ADDIE
Fat Boy	Faggot	Wop	Beanpole
Fatso	Fag	Greaser	Skyscraper
Fatty	Gay	Greaseball	Big Mouth
Blubber	Fairy	Slimeball	Show-off
Pork Chop	Queer	Guinea	Know-it-All
Dough Boy	Girl	Dummy	Brains
Dweeb	Sissy	Geek	Einstein
Nerd	Wimp	Schizo	Dweeb
Spaz	Wuss	Hooligan	Nerdette
Lardo	Pervert	J. D.	Godzilla
Lardass	Freak	Freak	Loser
Lardbar	Mutant	Ree-tard	
Fluff	Homo	Dweeb	
Roly-Poly	Dweeb	Scuz	
Dork	Dork	Dork	
Geek	Nerd	Loser	
Loser	Geek		
	Tinkerbell		
	Twinkletoes		
	TinkyWinky		
	Joanna		
	Josephine		
	JoJo		
	Jodi		
	Joannie		
	Loser		

Skeezie whistles. "Impressive, man. Are we awesome or what?"

We high-five it around the table, acting like this is a big joke, but we all know it isn't. Then another idea comes to me. I grab a clean napkin and write, Dweeb. Then I draw a big circle around it and a slash through it, so it ends up looking like this:

"Here's what we gotta do," I go on. "We take all these words and write each one on its own sheet of paper. Then we put a circle around it and a line through it and then we put them up all over school."

"And what do we say about the Freedom—I mean, the No-Name Party?" Addie asks.

I can't believe I have an answer for this. It's all coming to me, without my even having to think about it. "We don't say anything," I go. "Not at first. That's the beauty of it, see? Ms. Wyman won't even know there's another party in the running. Nobody will know. We'll keep the suspense going for a couple of days and then we'll hit the walls with posters for the No-Name Party. How're they going to stop us then?"

Addie is practically jumping up and down, she's so excited. She looks dangerously close to hugging me. "It's brilliant, Bobby," she says.

"There's a name for this," Joe gives. "Teaser advertising, I think it is. I *love* it! It's so . . . subverted."

"Subversive," says Addie.

"Show-off!" goes Joe.

"Twinkletoes!" Addie goes right back at him.

They both laugh, and Skeezie says to me, "I think *you* should run for president, man."

"Yeah, Bobby," Addie joins in, "this is *your* idea." ·

"No way," I tell them. "I'm not getting up in front of the whole school and giving a speech. I'm a behind-the-scenes kind of guy, okay?"

They can see I mean it, so they let it go. Then the Skeeze asks, "But how are we gonna convince DuShawn to go along with this?"

"Are you kidding?" Addie asks. "He's probably got a longer list of names than any of us."

We all nod, because what do we know, and Addie says she'll talk to him right after lunch.

Meanwhile, I'm having the biggest brainstorm yet. "Wait a minute, you guys, we have to have a slogan, right? What do you think of this: Sticks and stones may break our bones, but names will break our spirit."

I'm looking at them now, waiting for them to laugh, I don't know why, and they're looking at me like that's what they expected, too, that I'd come up with something funny. But what I've come up with is something other than funny. Something even better than funny. What I've come up with is the truth.

15

MONDAY NIGHT we're back at Joe's house, printing up names on his computer and drawing red circles around them and red slashes through them. Every time we put a slash through one of those names, it's like we're casting a vote for our own party.

It's just the Gang of Five this time. Kelsey's mom doesn't like her being out on school nights, and DuShawn, well, DuShawn got kind of weird when Addie and I talked to him about the new party idea. Not that I blame him. What it went like was this:

Addie: DuShawn, guess what? We've come up with a whole new approach to the Freedom Party. You're going to love it.

DuShawn: Cool.

Addie: It's called the No-Name Party, and what we need is a list of all the names you've ever been called.

DuShawn: Names?

Addie: Yes, names. Put-downs. You know what I'm talking about.

DuShawn: Uh-huh. I get your drift. You're thinkin' because I'm black I've been called names.

Addie: Haven't you?

DuShawn: No.

Me: Never?

DuShawn: No. I mean, I know there are bigots out there, okay. And maybe I'm just lucky, but I've never had to deal with it.

Addie: Well, but will you still run for president on our ticket?

DuShawn: Why do you want me to run, Addie?

Addie: I told you. You're smart and . . .

DuShawn: And black, you said so yourself.

Addie: Well, yes, I guess so, but that's not . . .

DuShawn: That's not what? You got no end to that sentence. And you got eyes that see no further than the color of my skin.

Me: Where are you going, DuShawn?

DuShawn: I'm going to think this over.

Addie: Well, but, you won't let us down, will you?

DuShawn: Who's lettin' who down, Addie? There's somethin' for *you* to think over.

"Do you think DuShawn's going to back out?" I ask Addie as I'm slashing a red line through KNOW-IT-ALL.

Addie shakes her head, exasperated. "I hope not," she goes. "I tried calling him before coming over here, but his sister said he wasn't home. I don't know why he's being so sensitive. He said himself that the color of his skin is just a fact. The way he said the color of my skin is—"

"Like peach ice cream," Skeezie pitches in. "Or was it the inside of almonds? The dude is a poet. I'll tell you something else, Addie: The dude likes you."

"What?!" Addie makes a mess of the circle she's drawing and crumples up LARDO.

"Print that one out again," I tell her. "It's one of my favorites."

"I do not know what you're talking about," she informs Skeezie, getting that tight-lipped look of hers that makes me think of Ms. Wyman. "There is no way

DuShawn Carter likes me. And I'm not saying that because I'm white and he's, you know . . ."

"The color of night," says the Skeeze.

"Shut *up!*" Addie goes. I am detecting her peach ice-cream cheeks turning the shade of raspberry sherbet. "I am saying he couldn't like me because he's always picking on me. Spitballs and whoopee cushions and last week he was poking me all through social studies. I could hardly—"

"Breathe?" I go, and Skeezie and Joe and I crack up.

"You guys! This is what I get for having three boys as my best friends."

"Count your blessings," says Joe. "Girls'd tease you worse. I mean, if we were *girls,* the whole *school* would know you like Colin by now."

Joe looks up from REE-TARD and goes, "Oops."

Silence takes over the room and holds us hostage. Addie glares first at Joe, then at Skeezie.

"You told," she says. "I can't believe you told."

Skeezie runs a hand through his hair. "I, uh, well, I didn't mean to, it just kind of came out."

"It just kind of came out? How lame is that? I can't believe you told them, Skeezie. You promised."

"Don't get mad at Skeezie," says Joe, "and, anyway, we're your friends, too. How come you're keeping secrets from us?"

All of a sudden it's Addie who looks like she's been caught. She glances down at FREAK and meticulously circles it.

"I thought you guys would laugh at me" is what she says when she finally speaks. "I've never liked a boy before."

"So?" Joe says. "Bobby likes a girl, nobody's laughing at him."

"Not to his face, anyways," says the Skeeze. I throw a marker at him.

Addie looks at me. You can see she's relieved to get the attention off her. "Who do you like?" she asks.

"Kelsey," I say, her name coming out like no big thing.

"Kelsey's nice," Addie says. "Quiet, but nice. Are you going to ask her to go out with you?"

"I don't know."

"Well, *I'm* going to ask Colin if he wants to go to the dance with me. That is, if a certain party who shall remain nameless but whose initials are Skeezie

147

Tookis ever comes through on certain promises he made."

"I *did* come through," Skeezie protests. "I put a note in his locker and I *told* you that tomorrow I'd put in another one. And, anyways, nobody asks anybody to the dance. You just go."

"Unless you're going *out* with somebody, then you go with that person," Addie says, like she's all of a sudden in charge of the rules of the world. "If I could just find out if he likes me, then I could ask if he wants to go out with me. And then we could go to the dance together."

I start humming "Someday My Prince Will Come," to which Skeezie and Joe pitch in their vocal contributions.

"I *knew* you'd laugh at me!" Addie cries. She stands up and, I swear on a stack of pancakes, stamps her foot. This really gets us to cracking up, and Addie yells, "Morons!"

"Morons!" goes the Skeeze. "That's one we forgot!"

"Cretins!" says Joe. "Numbskulls!"

"Idiots!" I yell. "Jerks!"

Addie can't help herself. She forgets her anger and joins in. "Birdbrains!" she hollers. "Turkeys! Chickens!"

"Now those are *really* foul names!" Skeezie says, and before you know it we're all whooping it up and running to the computer to add these names to all the others.

16

COVERING THE school with our handiwork takes planning, since we don't want anybody catching us at it. We don't even try putting the signs up before classes start, on account of Addie and me getting stopped the day before. Instead, we each stick a bunch of them in our binders, along with a roll of tape. Then we all find a reason to be excused from one class or another, sneak the papers and tape out from under our shirts, and get those signs up faster than Ms. Wyman changes moods. By some kind of miracle, not one of us gets caught. We think. By lunchtime, there are over sixty No-Name signs running along the corridors of Paintbrush Falls Middle School. It's all everybody's talking about.

Everybody, that is, but us.

This is because the minute the Skeeze opens his

mouth to say something, Addie shushes him so hard he practically tosses the dessert he's just stolen from her back on her tray.

"We can't talk about this here!" Addie admonishes the three of us. "We have to keep a low profile!"

Her words make me think she is maybe going into her business exec mode, but it turns out she's got more on her mind than the No-Name Party.

"So?" she asks Skeezie, leaning across the table and taking back the chocolate-chip cookie he is trying to hide from her.

"I took care of it," says the Skeeze. He squeezes the words out of the corner of his mouth like a hit man.

"Took care of what?" I ask.

Skeezie eyes Addie with a should-I-spill-the-beans look.

"Go ahead," Addie tells him. "They know anyway."

"Gee, trying to figure out what you two are talking about is as much fun as picking scabs," Joe gives, all sarcastic-like. "Tomorrow let's all bring decoder rings and we can send each other secret messages."

"Hardy, har," goes the Skeeze. Turning to Addie,

he says, "I put a note in his locker that says, 'The person who likes you will be waiting by the flagpole at three-fifteen.'"

Addie gets all bug-eyed and says, "Does this mean I actually have to show up? What am I going to say? What if there are other kids around? How will he know it's me?"

"Nobody hangs out by the flagpole, that's why I picked it. What you say is your business."

"I never knew you to be at a loss for words," I point out to Addie.

I'm expecting Joe to chime something in, too, but he's looking down at his lunch like he's not even in the room with us anymore. Then all of a sudden he comes back to life and says, "Oh, guess what? I found a note in *my* locker."

"I didn't put it there, I swear," says Skeezie.

"I wasn't worried," says Joe. "I *know* who it's from."

"Who?" asks Addie.

"Kelsey. Who else would it be?"

"Kelsey likes you?"

"Uh-huh."

"Oh."

"What did the note say?" I ask, not really sure I want to hear all the lovey-dovey stuff Kelsey is writing to Joe.

Joe pulls a neatly folded piece of paper out of his pocket and reads in his best going-for-an-Oscar movie-star voice, "'I wish I could be like you. If I were, I would tell you how I feel.'" He refolds the paper and goes, "Barf."

"That's it?" Addie asks.

Joe nods. "She's a girl of few words. What am I going to do, you guys? I don't want to hurt her feelings, but . . . Bobby, you like her, why don't you ask her to go out with you?"

"Oh, thanks," I say. "Just like that, I'm going to go up to her and say, 'Hi, I know you like my friend Joe and all, but will you go out with me? Let me remind you that you *did* smile at me one time for one-millionth of a second, and, oh, here's a major selling point: Joe doesn't like girls and I do.'"

Addie gets this serious look on her face. "You know, it's just possible that Kelsey *does* like you, Bobby. She could easily have mixed up your locker with Joe's. They're right next to each other."

"Forget it," I say.

"Yeah, you're probably right," says Addie. "She strikes me as the cautious type. She wouldn't make a mistake about something like that."

"Here's what you should do, Jo*Dan,*" goes the Skeeze, picking chocolate chips out of a cookie. I look down at my tray. My dessert is missing. "You should cool it with her. Y'know? You've been real chummy with her lately. You don't mean nothin' by it, but she's getting the wrong message, know what I mean? You gotta not encourage her."

"Gee," I say, "you should write an advice column for *The Easel.*" That's the name of our school paper. Do not ask.

"Dear Skeezie," Joe goes as the bell rings and we start picking up our trays whilst I snatch what's left of my cookie out of the Skeeze's mitt, "I am in love with this dynamite girl who sits next to me in social studies but I don't dare tell her because I've got this real bad zit on the tip of my nose and besides which I have b.o. and halitoshus . . ."

"Halitosis," Addie butts in.

"Whatever," goes Joe, scowling at her. "Anyway, I

cry myself to sleep every night because I am already twelve years old and have never known love. I do not want to die an old maid, or whatever it's called if you're a guy. Please help me, O great wise one of the seventh grade. Sincerely yours, Zit-Face Zach."

Skeezie clears his throat. "Dear Zit-Face, Find yourself a nice girl with zits and b.o. and bad breath. Believe me, they're out there. Good luck!"

From here the conversation plummets as we start heaving truly gross made-up letters at Skeezie and he tosses back replies that are in such bad taste we have no choice but to make barf noises, when all of a sudden we stop talking altogether and get to listening with all our ears because there is this sort of buzz going on around us. Everybody's saying, "Who put these signs up?" And some of the kids are quoting the words and laughing, but others are quoting them and saying stuff like, "I was called that in fourth grade and I really hated it."

We listen to hear if anybody's figured out who put them on the walls, and to our surprise most of what we hear is conjecture that it's the school itself that's behind it. Nobody figures it has anything to do with the student council elections or the group formerly know as the Freedom Party.

"This is so cool," Joe says, and Addie shushes him and Joe calls her Wendy and she swats him and he swats back and Skeezie goes, "Girls!" and they both turn and swat him, and Mrs. DePaolo, who happens to be walking by just then with a sweater draped over her shoulders, says, "None of that now." And we all go, "It's okay, Mrs. DePaolo."

By the end of the day, we are all agreeing that what's happening is pretty cool. The plan is that we will let the signs stay up one more day and then on Thursday we'll hit the walls with posters for the No-Name Party.

Right now, though, it's time for me to get to Awkworth & Ames, and I'm at my locker stuffing my backpack while Addie is chittering away behind me like a nervous bird, asking the time every five seconds because she's worried about timing her appearance at the flagpole just right, when all of a sudden DuShawn and Tonni are in our faces and DuShawn is going, "Addie, I got to talk with you."

And at the same moment, Ms. Wyman pops her head out of the door and calls out, "Ms. Carle, a word with you, please."

Panic takes over Addie's features like a rash.

"Addie," says DuShawn, "I've been thinking—"

"DuShawn is *out*," Tonni goes, finishing the sentence for him.

"Let *me* tell it!" DuShawn says, to which Tonni rolls her eyeballs.

"You're dropping out?" says Addie. "You can't drop out."

"Who says I can't?" DuShawn gives back, looking like he's just been waiting for something to get angry about. "Tonni's right about you. She says you're just—"

"What's Tonni got to do with this?" says Addie. "Can't you think for yourself, DuShawn?"

"I *am* thinking for myself. And I don't want to run on your fool ticket, okay? That's the bottom line, okay?"

"Tell it," Tonni mutters, and she takes hold of DuShawn's elbow. "Let's go, DuShawn. Come on, we're outta here."

Addie clicks her tongue and is about to say something else when Ms. Wyman gives her a holler again, and Addie asks me the time again and I tell her to get a watch, but give her the time, anyway, which is five minutes past three, and she says, "Please, please go to the flagpole and tell Colin to wait." But I cannot do this on account of my job, and fortunately she does not ask Joe or Skeezie on account of Ms. Wyman is out in the hall now, advancing, and Addie is saying, "I'm coming, Ms. Wyman. I'm coming."

With one last look at us, she mouths, "Forum. Five-thirty."

To which we all nod as she disappears into the ogre's lair.

Skeezie turns to Joe and says, "Sorry."

"About what?"

"Fixing Addie up with Colin and all."

"I told you it was okay," Joe goes.

"Hey," says the Skeeze, "I've got an idea. Maybe *you* should go meet Colin at the flagpole."

To which Joe says, "So funny I forgot to laugh."

17

Addie: Okay, okay, I know we have to talk about
            what we're going to do now that DuShawn
            has dropped out, but I have got to tell you
            what happened with Colin. It is too amazing!

Skeezie: What's amazing is that you manage to talk so
            fast and write everything down at the same
            time. How do you do that? Hey, look who's
            working here today. It's HellomynameisSteffi.
            Maybe we'll actually get our food before—

Addie: Skeezie! I am trying to tell you something.

Bobby: I've got something to tell, too.

Addie: Okay, but me first. Please, you guys. Please.

Joe: Begging is so not you, Addison. But go
            ahead.

Skeezie: Yeah, shoot. Addison, huh? I forgot that's
            your real name.

Addie: That's right, <u>Schuyler</u>. Anyway, let me tell, will you? So after I got through talking to Ms. Wyman, who only wanted to talk <u>math</u> with me, for heaven's sake, like <u>that</u> couldn't wait until tomorrow, well, I was a few minutes late getting to the flagpole, and Colin was walking away, so I—

Joe: Did you tell him the notes were from you? About you, I mean?

Addie: No, I never mentioned the notes. He was leaving, so I walked faster, you know, to catch up, and then I said, "Oh, hi, Colin," like it's just coincidence or something that we're meeting there.

Skeezie: That doesn't make sense.

Addie: Well, I didn't want to appear <u>desperate</u>.

Joe: Dear Skeezie, Today I ran after a boy as he was trying to get away. I tackled him and we both landed in the mud. Do you think I appeared desperate?

Addie: Ignoring you, I go on. So he said, "Oh, hi, Addie."

Joe: It's good you're writing this down. The
            dialogue so far is priceless.

Addie: Still ignoring you. So I say, "What are you
            doing here?" And he says, "Oh, I was just
            waiting for somebody." And I say, "Oh,
            really?" And he says, "Uh-huh." So then
            I'm thinking, "What do I say now?" But
            he says, "Do you want to walk together?"
            Could you die?

Skeezie: Wow, what is that? Like first base or
            something, walking together?

Addie: You're jealous.

Skeezie: Not a chance.

Addie: So we're walking and he tells me he thinks
            that I'm the one behind the signs that are up
            around school and he says he thinks it's
            really great and he thinks I'm the smartest
            girl in the whole class and he really respects
            me, like my stand on the Pledge of Allegiance
            and all, and then he asks me if it's true.

Skeezie: All right! Here's our food.

Joe: What's true?

Addie: About me being behind the signs that are up and all. So I swear him to secrecy and I tell him that it is true, and then I tell him about the No-Name Party and then he swears me to secrecy and says that even though he wants Drew to win—and himself, of course—that he also hopes I win, because he thinks I deserve to. And then . . . and then . . .

Joe: Take a breath, Addie. And chew your food.

Addie: And then I ask him if he wants to stop at the Candy Kitchen—I can't believe I had the nerve—to have a soda or ice cream or something, and he says he can't but maybe another time. And then we said goodbye. I can't _believe_ it. I'm actually _going out_ with Colin Briggs!

Bobby: What makes you think you're going out with him?

Addie: Please. 1. He showed up. 2. He gave me all these compliments. 3. He said he'd go with me another time for a soda or ice cream. What more is there?

Skeezie: You're lovesick, girl, and it is not a pretty
sight. And these stinkin' french fries are
cold. Hey, hey, you, HellomynameisSteffi.

Addie: Skeezie, <u>stop</u> snapping your fingers!

Skeezie: I'm telling you, this place has gone down
the toilet ever since they took out the
jukebox.

Bobby: You know what I don't understand? Why is
it suddenly such a big deal to be going out
with somebody? It's such <u>pressure</u>.

Skeezie: I'm not going out with anybody. Ever. Except
maybe HellomynameisSteffi. If she brings me
hot french fries, I might even ask her to
marry me. Anyway, Addie, I'm happy for
you. Seriously. Because that's what you
want, right? To go out with Colin.

Addie: And <u>you</u> helped, Skeezie! You are <u>such</u> a
good friend. I hope you'll know what it's like
someday.

Skeezie: What?

Addie: Love.

Skeezie: Not interested. Sorry.

Hellomy nameis Steffi:	You snapped?
Skeezie:	Yeah, like five minutes ago. These french fries are cold.
Hellomy nameis Steffi:	Well, we can't have that, can we, Elvis? Here, hand me that plate and I'll get you some fresh ones.
Skeezie:	Honest? Wow. Will you marry me?
Hellomy nameis Steffi:	I don't know. Are you smart or just cute?
Skeezie:	I, uh, uh . . .
Hellomy nameis Steffi:	You think on that while I get your fries.
Skeezie:	What? What are you looking at?
Addie:	You. Just seeing what Mr. I'm-Never-Going-to-Fall-in-Love looks like when he falls in love.
Skeezie:	What makes you think I'm in love?
Addie:	And I quote: "I, uh, uh . . ."
Skeezie:	Get out.
Joe:	Hey, guys, can we get down to business? I need to get home.

Addie:	Sure, of course. I'm sorry, I just couldn't help . . . I just <u>had</u> to tell you. You're my best friends.
Joe:	I know. And I'm happy for you, too, Addie. Really. You and Colin, you make a nice couple.
Addie:	Thanks, Joe.
Skeezie:	So about the Lame-Brain Party . . .
Addie:	Stop calling it that. That's the whole point: No names!
Skeezie:	Right. Sorry.
Addie:	Well, we have to come up with a candidate for president by tomorrow, so we can get our posters up on Thursday. I was thinking about asking Royal, but—
Bobby:	I don't think that's a good idea.
Addie:	Do you have a better one?
Bobby:	I think <u>you</u> should run for president. And, Joe, you should run for vice president.
Joe:	Me? I'm not big on politics.
Bobby:	Come on. What could make more sense than the Gang of Five running on the same ticket together? Look at all the names we came up

with for the signs we put up. Those are <u>our</u> names. <u>We</u> are the No-Name Party!

Addie: You're right. It's brilliant, Bobby. Joe, please say yes.

Joe: Will I have to do anything?

Addie: Nothing more than you're doing already. And if we're elected, well, then you have to go to student council meetings, I guess. Oh, please say yes, Joe. It will be fun.

Joe: Okay. All right. Who knows, maybe it will be the start of my meteoric rise to stardom!

Bobby: A toast to the No-Name Party!

Hellomy nameis Steffi: Hot french fries comin' through! There you go—hot fries for the hot dude!

Skeezie: Stanks.

Hellomy nameis Steffi: What?

Joe: What did you say?

Bobby: You said stanks!

Skeezie: I said thanks.

Joe: You said stanks.

Addie: Look, Skeezie's blushing.

Skeezie: Am not.

Hellomy
nameis
Steffi: You guys need anything else? What about

you, Elvis? Still want to marry me?

Skeezie: Huh?

Hellomy
nameis
Steffi: Forgot already, huh? You cute guys are all

the same. All talk, no action. Okay, seriously,

I hope those fries are hot enough for you.

You guys holler if you need anything else.

Addie: Skeezie's in lo-o-o-ve!

Skeezie: Shut up with that!

Joe: You are so blushing.

Skeezie: I am so not.

Joe: Hey, Skeezie, pass the ketchup, will ya?

Skeezie: Here ya go.

Joe: Stanks.

Skeezie: Very funny. You guys can stop laughing now.

Bobby: Sorry, Skeeze, but it is funny.

Addie: Really. Oh, Bobby, you had something you

wanted to tell.

Bobby: Oh, it's not that important. Just, my boss wasn't at work today and I waited on four customers and made <u>three</u> sales. And not just ties, either. Junior, he's the guy who was filling in for Mr. K—he said I was a really good salesman. And you know what? I think I am. Selling is fun. I might even want to do it when I grow up.

Skeezie: So what happened to the Grim Reaper?

Bobby: Mr. Kellerman? Oh, his mother—

Skeezie: Guy doesn't look like he <u>has</u> a mother.

Bobby: Well, he does. Did. She died yesterday. That's why he was out of work today. His mother—

Addie: Oh, gee.

Bobby: Yeah. She died.

18

I GET to thinking about this on the walk home. "This" being the fact that Mr. Kellerman's mother died. It is weird thinking about the way I just tossed that into the conversation back there at the Candy Kitchen, like, *Oh, yeah, by the way, somebody's life ended yesterday please pass the salt.* I mean, the man's mother died. She was a person.

I remember when it happened to me. I was seven, almost eight. Life was going along like normal, you know? My dad was working for the same nursery he works for now and my mom was an actress. She wasn't a famous actress or anything. She hardly made a living at it. Mostly, she did community theater and taught a few classes. Sometimes she would go out on the road for a couple of months, if she got a part in something, or do a show in Albany, which isn't that far away, or fly down to New York City for a day or two to shoot a commercial. She told me once that she had agreed to marry my dad and live in Paintbrush Falls as long as he didn't make her give up her dreams. She always told me to follow my dreams, too, do whatever it was that made me happy.

My dad was never much of a dreamer. He let my mom do the dreaming for the two of them. It was on account of her that he tried to get his own landscaping business going. I remember how excited he got talking about it at dinner some nights. My mom would sit there with her eyes glued on him, as if listening to him talk about what kind of shrubs did best in what kind of soil was the most fascinating thing in the whole world.

They were happy.

I was happy back then, too. I liked school. I wasn't fat yet.

Then one day my mom picked me up after school —I was in the second grade; it was April, I think— and my shoes were muddy, but she didn't tell me to scrape them off first the way she usually did. So I didn't, because I figured she must have her reasons, like maybe—in my seven-year-old mind, this made sense—maybe she *wanted* some mud in the car for a change. So I jumped in the car, mud and all, and she said, "How was your day, sweetie?" but there was something wrong with her voice, like she'd fallen on it and flattened the air out of it. I looked up at her and said, "Fine." I remember I was mad at Addie because she had told the teacher I'd been picking my nose and sticking the boogers under my chair and Mrs. Esley had scolded me and hadn't said one word to Addie about being a tattletale. Talk about no justice. Well, the point is that when I looked over and saw my mom's face, I didn't say a word about it, even though it had been the first thing I'd wanted to tell her. I could see something was wrong, and whatever it was, was a whole lot bigger than having your friend rat on you to your teacher.

I didn't ask what was going on. I didn't know how. I was only seven. What I found out later was that a couple of hours before she picked me up she had learned she had cancer.

She got sick really fast, so they couldn't hide the truth from me for long. My dad would have lied to me the whole time, I think, but my mom convinced him that I should know.

It's funny, my mom was always the one putting the big smiley face on everything. Everything was always going to be better in the morning. The glass was always half full. Anything was possible. Even when she would look in the mirror and groan about putting on weight (she had a sweet tooth, same as me) or get real angry after she'd lost an acting job, she'd find a way to turn things around and look on the bright side. My dad was just the opposite. He didn't even see the point in trying most of the time, so it was kind of a miracle that he was actually going to start his own business. Of course, the miracle was my mom.

When she got sick, my dad acted like it wasn't happening at first. He kept telling me she was getting better, but it wasn't because he wanted to protect me, as much as he wanted to believe it himself. My mom, she told me the truth straight out. She told me she was going to die, but that she would always be alive in my heart and that I would always have my dad and my dreams.

The summer between second and third grade, she was in the hospital most of the time. My dad began staying overnight there with her. I stayed with Addie and her mom and dad. One morning while we were sitting there eating breakfast, my dad showed up at the door, his face looking like it had caved in, like it was in ruins or something. Addie's mom said, "Oh, Mike," and she jumped up and held on to him while his knees gave out.

I can't remember if I cried. I just remember Addie's dad squatting down in front of me and asking me if I understood that my mom had died, and me saying yes, and then asking when was she coming home.

So I'm thinking about all this as I'm closing in on Shadow Glen Trailer Park, pondering how Mr. Kellerman has had his mom go and die on him, too, and wondering if maybe—even though he's a grown man and his mom was an old lady and all—just maybe he feels the way I did, knowing his mom has died but waiting for her to come home.

My dad is standing by the phone when I walk in, and he greets me with, "Know what I'm making for dinner?"

"A call to Pizza Place?" I go. "I want pepperoni."

"You got it," he says, and starts hitting the buttons.

There's a lot I could tell him, a lot that's on my mind, but what comes out when we're sitting there with our slices and the salad he's made because he tries to make sure I get balanced meals, is this:

"Dad, when did you start going out with girls?"

He laughs. "I've been wondering when we'd have this conversation."

I roll my eyes. "Daaad, I just asked you a simple question."

"I had my first girlfriend when I was ten," he tells me.

I am shocked to hear this. "Ten?" I go. "What were you? Some kind of fiend?"

"Why do you say that, Skip? I just liked this girl and I told her so. We decided to be boyfriend and girlfriend. That's all. It was simple then. I don't think we ever actually went out or anything. We played together. She liked sports. We had a good time."

"But *ten,*" I repeat, apparently unable to process a simple piece of information. "I'm twelve. Is there something wrong with me?"

This gets my dad laughing so hard he puts his hand up to his mouth to keep the pizza in.

"Glad I amuse you," I go.

Eventually, he calms down, but his eyes are all watery.

"I hope you realize I am humiliated," I tell him.

"No, no," he goes, the way parents do when they try to tell you you're wrong about something you happen to have firsthand experience of.

"I am," I say.

"Okay, I'm sorry, it's just . . . Skip, you're twelve. Good grief, you're just a kid."

"But you were ten."

"So? Like I say, it was easier then, simpler. Nobody thought it was a big deal to call somebody your girlfriend. But I had friends who didn't have their first girlfriend until they were in high school. Grady Buckower, know who I mean?"

I nod. Grady was my troop leader for the eight months I managed being a Cub Scout.

"Grady didn't have a girlfriend until he was in college—and then he married her! So what's behind all the questions?"

I thought, *How do I tell my dad I like a girl?*

"You like a girl, is that it?" he goes. "And you don't know if she likes you. Am I right?"

"Oh, I *know*," I tell him. "I know she *doesn't* like me. Well, what I mean is, I'm not so sure she *doesn't* like me, but I am sure she likes somebody else. But the somebody else doesn't like her, I mean, not as a girlfriend, he only likes her as a friend, so how do I let her know that I like her as, like, girlfriend material, and then what do I do if she laughs in my face, which I don't think this particular girl will do, but you never know, she might get hysterical."

My dad shoves a slice of pizza in his mouth, and I bet anything he is doing it to stifle a laugh. When I am a father, I swear on a stack of pancakes I will never laugh at my children.

I wait for him to chew and swallow.

"Think you can keep it under control now?" I ask.

"Cut me a little slack," he tells me. "I'm only

human. Look, kiddo, the direct approach is best. Hard as it is, just go up to the girl and tell her you like her. You don't have to ask her to be your girlfriend or anything, not right off the bat. Just say, 'I like you. Do you want to get together sometime?' Why not include her with your gang when you go to the Candy Kitchen?"

I think this over and figure it is not bad advice. I say, "It's a good thing I'm a boy."

This one really takes him by surprise. Me, too, for that matter.

"If I were a girl," I explain, "then I'd be missing Mom even more than I do, because I'd be at an age where I'd need, you know, to talk with a woman about stuff. But I'm a boy, so I've got my dad to talk to about guy stuff."

My dad looks like he's having trouble swallowing. He nods his head, slowly.

"Yep," he goes, "we're lucky we've got each other, all right."

I tell him then about Mr. Kellerman's mom dying and he tells me he heard, on account of it being a small town and news travels fast. And this gets us to talking about my mom dying, which I guess is what I really wanted to talk about all along. We do not talk about this often, not because my dad won't discuss it, more because what is there to say?

This time I think of something.

"How come after Mom died," I ask, pushing the uneaten lettuce and cucumbers and tomatoes around my plate, "you gave up on starting your own landscaping business?"

He answers this so fast I know he has thought about it before.

"I needed her," he says. "I'm not real good on my own."

"Don't say that, Dad. You *are* good."

He looks over and shakes his head at me. "That's just what your mom would have said. You're so much like her."

"You always tell me that," I say.

And this is when it hits me. No matter how many times I have heard my dad tell me I am just like my mom, I have always thought I was just like him—a get-along guy, somebody who doesn't want to make waves, who doesn't know how to dream for himself. All of a sudden, I'm thinking maybe I *am* more like my mom, not just a dreamer but somebody who can make things happen.

How do I describe what happens next? I am sitting there, looking at my dad while he chews at the skin around his right thumbnail, a bad habit he picked up around the time my mom got sick. And all of a sudden I feel sorry for him, because I see how different we are. No, not *how* different we are, just that we are different. That I am going to grow up, and what is going to happen to him?

"How come you don't date?" I ask.

He shrugs and starts in on his index finger. "I guess I just lost interest. That, and I don't have the energy for it. It's hard, you know, taking care of you and working and all. I don't have much room for fun."

"That's a cop-out," I say.

"Listen to who's the authority all of a sudden. Weren't you the guy who two minutes ago—"

"Right, two minutes ago I was asking advice about

how to talk to girls. But why should I listen to you, when you're too scared to ask a girl out yourself?"

"That's not fair," he says to me. "When you're older—"

"When I'm older I don't want to stop living if something bad happens to me. I don't want to give up. And I don't want my kid feeling sorry for me either."

If I were my dad, I probably would have yelled at me right about then. I would have slammed the table and said, "Don't you talk to me like that!" But I don't give my dad a chance to say anything. I just open up my lungs and gasp in a whole big wad of air and when I let it out, I start sobbing. Hard. So what is my dad to do? He comes around to my side of the table and gets a good grip on my shoulders and holds on to me tight and says, "It's okay, Skip, you just let it out. You and me, we haven't had a good cry in a long time."

And before we clear the table that night and before we play a hand of casino, that is just what we do. Dad and me. Hammer and Skip. We have a good cry.

19

WEDNESDAY MORNING all the signs are gone.

"I am telling you," Addie informs me as quick as she can latch onto my arm after I enter the school premises, "it's Ms. Wyman."

"I doubt it," I say. "It's probably Mr. Kiley. I don't mean Mr. Kiley himself, but, you know, the *school*. You have to have *permission* to put stuff up on the walls, which we did not exactly get."

"Well, I'm going to say something," goes Addie.

"Such as?"

"Such as didn't anybody ever hear of the First Amendment?"

It is my turn to latch onto an arm, which I do with hers. "Stop making everything a federal case," I tell her. "All we've got to do is let the school in on what we're doing. I say we go to Mr. Kiley and—"

"Ms. Carle, Mr. Goodspeed."

Ms. Wyman is standing there all of a sudden with her hands on her hips like a cop who's pulled us over, except there was no siren to warn us. Addie almost collides with her and I do a quick study of the two of them, both tall with big bones and their hair cut short almost the same way. If I wasn't so sure Addie is going to grow up to become the head of some big company or president of the United States or something, I swear in looking at the two of them I'm seeing Addie's future.

As Ms. Wyman commences to speak, she forms her mouth into the perfect imitation of a smile. "May I ask the two of you to hurry at your lockers this morning so that I may have a word with you before homeroom?"

I note that Addie is about to say something, probably along the lines of, "Until the homeroom bell rings, we are private citizens and you have no right to tell us what to do with our time," so I gently coincide the tip of my foot with the bony part of her ankle and the only word that comes out of her mouth is "ouch."

"That hurt!" Addie complains as Ms. Wyman walks away, chirping at other kids in the hall like they're Munchkins and she's Glinda, the Good Witch of the North.

"Sorry," I tell Addie, "I just didn't want you saying anything that was going to make her want second helpings of our livers. We're already in enough trouble."

"Trouble?" Addie goes. "For what? We didn't do anything wrong!"

Ms. Wyman doesn't see it this way.

"I just don't understand why you can't work within the system," she is telling us minutes later. We are standing in front of her desk.

"I don't know what you're talking about," Addie goes. One career option I rule out for her is diplomat.

"Don't play games with me, Ms. Carle," Ms. Wyman snaps back. Addie and I jump like it's a rubber band she's snapped at us. "You know perfectly well that you are behind those signs that were put up around school yesterday. There is no use denying it. You were seen by a teacher, who reported you to Mr. Kiley. I am not here to debate the worthiness of the message. I am here to remind you that you were told there is no need for a third party and therefore there *is* no third party."

"Who says the signs had anything to do with a third party?" Addie jumps in with both feet before I can stop her. "What about freedom of speech, freedom of expression?"

Ms. Wyman's sigh is like a blanket she pulls over her on a cold morning. Addie is the cold morning; you can tell Ms. Wyman just wishes she would go away.

"Ms. Wyman," I say. "Do you think we could talk to Mr. Kiley about this?"

"Mr. Kiley asked me to speak with you," Ms. Wyman goes.

"It's true that the signs have to do with a third party," I tell her, fast, so she can't get another word in and, besides, I am hoping the truth will disarm her. "But it's different from the Freedom Party—and it's different from the other two parties, too. It has a message that *needs* to be heard. I'm sorry we didn't get permission to put the signs up. We know we should have. Sometimes kids just act impulsively, but it's because we have strong feelings, not because we're trying to make trouble."

Ms. Wyman's mouth is slightly open, like she's ready at a moment's notice to put it to work, but she doesn't say anything. I can tell that she is actually listening. Addie must realize this, too, because she doesn't jump in with her own ready-for-action mouth and lets me keep talking.

"Maybe we could meet with you *and* Mr. Kiley," I go on. "If you would just hear what it is we're trying to do, you'd understand about the signs. Will you do that, Ms. Wyman, please? Just hear us."

Ms. Wyman gives me a good study then, looking me over the way *I* look people over—except not when they know I'm looking—as if she's trying to see what's on the inside even more than what's on the outside.

"Bobby," she says, "you are full of surprises this morning. You're usually so quiet."

"Yes, ma'am," I say.

"And you're very convincing in your sincerity as

well as your words. I will speak to Mr. Kiley and will let you know if we'll meet with you."

"*If?*" Addie goes, and I reintroduce my toe and her ankle.

"That's great," I tell Ms. Wyman. "Thank you. Thank you so much."

"Doesn't she think *I'm* sincere?" Addie hisses at me as we move away from Ms. Wyman's desk.

"Or you could say, 'That was so cool, Bobby. Way to go,'" I point out and leave her with that thought as we turn away from each other to take our seats.

The meeting takes place during lunch period. I do not know how it is that Ms. Wyman decided from the beginning that I was as involved as Addie, but it is a good thing she did because if I had not been at the meeting, the No-Name Party would have had a shorter life span than a fruit fly.

Addie doesn't even wait for her fanny to hit the chair before she starts talking. "Mr. Kiley," she says, "it's not fair that our signs were taken down. What they represent is important! And what about freedom of—"

"Stop," Mr. Kiley says without raising his voice. He folds shut an appointment book and rolls up the sleeves of his shirt. I note that he has managed a much better coordination of shirt and tie today, although the jacket slung over the back of a nearby chair is a disaster, haberdasherily speaking.

Ms. Wyman clears her throat. "As I explained to you, Mr. Kiley," she says, "it was Bobby's argument that convinced me we should have this meeting. Perhaps *he* should be the one to speak."

"It's a free country," Mr. Kiley says. "Either one of you can speak—Bobby, Addie. I just don't want to hear anything more about what's fair or not fair. I want to hear specifics. I want to know what it is you are doing and why you think you should be allowed to do it."

"You just said yourself it's a free country," Addie says. Fastest mouth in the west. Or anywhere else, for that matter. "Well, why shouldn't—"

"Did I not just say this is what I *don't* want to hear?" Mr. Kiley says. "You know, Addie, ever since you started this business of refusing to say the Pledge, I have sensed in you a rebel without a cause."

"But—"

"Uh-uh-uh. I want to hear *specifics*."

"Mr. Kiley," I butt in, hoping to head Addie off, "I

have been called names ever since third grade, on account of my being, y'know, chunky. My friends have been called names, too. So have a lot of other kids. The other day, Daryl Williams was called a name—"

"Dweeb," Addie interjects.

"Right. And I thought—I mean, *we* thought—that that shouldn't be allowed. So we came up with the idea of the No-Name Party. And that's what makes us different from the other parties. That's what our platform is about—making kids think about name-calling and, well, putting an end to it, if we can. We put up those signs yesterday to get everybody talking about it. And it worked."

Mr. Kiley nods his head. I take it to mean, "Go on." But I'm not sure what else I have to say. I open my mouth again and hope for the best.

"Addie wanted to start a third party because she believes that we have a long way to go in this country until there is real justice and liberty for all. *That's* why she stopped saying the Pledge, Mr. Kiley, not because she's a rebel without a cause—although that *is* a good movie."

I note out of the corner of my occuli that this gets a

smile—a real smile—from both moviegoers of the older generation. I press on.

"The problem with the Freedom Party was that it wasn't specific enough. Even saying we represented minorities didn't mean a whole lot. But saying we want to put an end to kids being called names, well, that does have meaning. And you have to admit it would make a difference. I mean, you don't have to admit anything, I'm not telling you what to do, I just mean—"

Mr. Kiley's expression stops me. I can tell that he has heard enough and that I've won. I'm thinking, I really *am* a good salesman. Thinking I am good at something makes me smile, I can't help myself.

"Very impressive, Bobby," Mr. Kiley goes. "I wish I could say that school policy had put an end to the kind of name-calling you're talking about, but it hasn't. I'm sure Ms. Wyman would agree with me—knowing how much she cares about self-esteem—that anything you can do among your peers would be of great help. I want to give the No-Name Party the go-ahead. What do you say, Ms. Wyman?"

I look over at Ms. Wyman and she is looking at

me, like one human being looking at another, and it strikes me how funny it is that grown-ups, especially in school, always call each other Mr. This and Ms. That. And I think how different it would be to call Ms. Wyman Ellen, which is her first name, and Mr. Kiley Tim, which is his first name, and I get to wondering what Mr. Kellerman's first name is. You would think I would have more important things to think about at this particular moment, but this is how my mind works.

Ms. Wyman brings me back to reality.

"You've presented a very compelling argument," she says to me. "Good luck."

I cannot believe it. The No-Name Party is in business, and all on account of me. As we are leaving the office, I am worried that Addie will be mad at me. After all, this whole thing was her idea and it is starting to feel like I have taken it away from her.

But she isn't mad. Not at all. What she says when we get in the clear is, "That was so cool, Bobby. Way to go."

THE NEXT day our posters are up all over the walls—
and they stay up. No dolphins this time. Our symbol
has become a name in a circle with a line slashed
through it. This is what one of the posters looks like:

Vote for the NO-NAME PARTY—
End name-calling once and for all!
President . . . Addie Carle
Vice President . . . Joe Bunch
Treasurer . . . Bobby Goodspeed
Secretary . . . Skeezie Tookis

Løser

Sticks and Stones May Break Our Bones,
But Names Will Break Our Spirit

You might figure—*we* did, anyway—that putting our names out there like that, especially with certain choice epithets right underneath them, would make us sitting targets for ridicule. But it doesn't happen. I mean, what can anybody say that doesn't just prove our point? Even Kevin Hennessey is at a loss for words. All he can come up with is, "Whatsa matter? Didja run out of whales to save?" Not exactly A-material, even for him.

Between science and math, Daryl Williams smiles at me in the hall. I want to tell him how he was the inspiration for the whole thing, but I don't want to embarrass him, so I just smile back.

In art class on Friday, Colin tells Joe and me that he thinks what we're doing is the best thing that ever happened at P.F.M.S., he *means* it, and that Addie is *amazing,* and then he turns to Joe and goes, "Hey, we're running against each other for vice president. Is it bad if I vote for *you?*" and Joe blushes on every part of him that shows. This gets me feeling sorry for Joe and wondering what Colin would do if he knew Joe liked him.

I decide that after about the age of three, life is not simple.

Which reminds me.

On Thursday, Joe gets another note from Kelsey in his locker. It says, "Meet me at the flagpole after school."

To which Addie goes, "At least she could be original." She owns up to having told Kelsey about meeting Colin there on Tuesday and how they're now going out together. If she's looking to spread gossip, Kelsey-the-silent is the wrong person to tell.

Anyway, Joe begs Addie and me to go with him to the flagpole after school on account of Skeezie is unavailable and Joe does not want to be a creep and not show up, and besides which he figures he has to tell her to her face that he does not want to go out with her and he needs our support. He thinks he is doing some kind of community service or something when he turns to me and says, "And if *you're* there, Bobby, you can walk her home and console her and then maybe she'll decide she likes *you*."

"Great idea," I tell him. "I can be like the year's

supply of steak sauce they give you when you don't win the sports car."

It turns out that Joe does not have to tell her anything and I do not have to be the steak sauce, because Kelsey chickens out and doesn't show. Leastwise, that is what we figure. What happens is that we go to the flagpole after school and wait until all of a sudden Addie spots Colin and goes, "Oo, my boyfriend," and runs off. At which point I turn to Joe and make some comment along the lines of, "I hope Addie's brain does not completely rot out on us before the election." And Joe says, "Do you think Colin is going to start hanging out with us?" To which I shrug because I do not have an answer.

Joe watches Colin and Addie walk away and I almost—but don't—reach over and rub him on the top of his head, because he reminds me of one of those puppies who looks up at you at the pet store with its big, sad eyes, just begging you to take it home with you, but nobody does.

It is bad enough watching Joe being miserable and Addie being happy, even though I can't help wonder-

ing how seriously Colin takes his relationship with
Addie, or if he even knows he has one. To make matters worse, I find this scrap of paper after art class
on Friday when I am on cleanup. It is all crumpled up
and for some reason I do not know the meaning of,
I uncrumple it and there I discover the initials B. C.
inside a heart. I do not think anything of this until,
upon closer inspection, I see that the C is a G and I am
all of a sudden confronted with the mystery of who in
my art class likes me, because of course I am figuring
these to be my initials. I am wishing it is Kelsey but
I know it is not, so I get to casting my eyes around the
room without being too obvious about it when Mr.
Minelli calls out, "Looking for something, Bobby?"
and I drop all these scraps of paper on the floor and
sputter some kind of answer that must be pretty funny
because it gets a lot of people laughing, but for the
life of me I have no idea what it is I say.

Walking to my job, I contemplate life in a mona-
stery.

I think at least I won't have to deal with Mr. Kellerman today because his mother just died and why

would he not give himself a few days off to feel sad in the privacy of his own home? That is the normal course of things, I figure. But Mr. K is not your normal individual, so not only is he there when I step into the tie department to select my neckwear for the next two hours, but he greets me with a snappish, "You are five minutes late, Mr. Goodspeed!"

I have not given a whole lot of thought to what I would say to Mr. Kellerman the next time I saw him. I know I should say something about his mother dying, along the lines of, "I'm sorry your mother died." That's just good form. But his jabbing at me about being late does not leave me much room for wanting to be nice. So I just mumble *sorry* under my breath, grab a tie, and head to the stockroom to put it on.

For the next hour, Mr. Kellerman hardly says a word to me. Mostly he fusses with piles of clothes the way he usually does, muttering under his breath, and glancing up at the clock. I glance there, too, from time to time, because it is natural that I am eager for my break to arrive, especially as today has been another no-show day, in terms of customers. As I see the big hand about to hit the twelve, I am all set to say, "I'm going for a break," when it occurs to me Mr. Kellerman is nowhere in sight. And at the same moment who should appear but a customer.

He is a man about my grandfather's age or maybe older. He squints at me as if he has never seen a twelve-year-old tie salesman before, which I venture to say he has not, and when I ask if I may be of assistance, as per page something-or-other of the six stapled pages, he looks around as if trying to spot the spaceship in which I arrived.

"You're awfully young," he goes. I acknowledge the truth of what he is saying, but tell him that I am trained and ready to be of service.

"Usually, Mr. Kellerman helps me," he grumbles, letting me know that the service I am trained and ready to provide will not be required.

"I'll go get him," I say, and then think to ask the man his name.

"Mr. Mars," he says. I think this is pretty funny, having just had the alien thing going on in my head, but I keep my amusement to myself.

The stockroom is eerily silent. Every time I put my foot down, the floor creaks. "Mr. Kellerman?" I go in a hushed voice like I've just stepped into an alternate universe. The theme to *The Blair Witch Project* starts playing in my head. I have not seen *The Blair Witch Project,* so I do not know if in fact what I am hearing is the theme, but I imagine this is what it must sound like, this creepy music I've got going in my cranium as I make my way down shadowy aisles piled high with boxes, breathlessly anticipating some lunatic with hollow eyes and an ax jumping out at me at any moment. I am wondering if my mother's mind worked the way mine does, and if that's why she was an actress, and what I will be. That is, if I survive the attack of the murderous fiend who is lurking behind men's dress shirts, sizes 15 1/2 to 17, to my right.

As it turns out, there is no murderous fiend lurking there, but there is someone. He does not hear me at first, just as I do not hear him. His back is to me, his left hand stretched out to hold on to a shelf, his right hand dangling at his side. If I didn't know it was Mr. Kellerman, I might really be spooked, on account of that creepy music going in my mind a few minutes back, because the way he is bent forward he almost looks headless.

I clear my throat and say, "Mr. Kellerman?"

He jumps a little at the sound of my voice, but doesn't turn to face me. "What are you doing here?" he says. "We can't both be on break at the same time. You should be out on the floor."

"I know that, Mr. Kellerman. But there's a man, a customer—"

"Well, take care of him!" he barks at me.

"But he asked for you, Mr. Kellerman. It's Mr. Mars."

Mr. Kellerman heaves a big sigh and slowly turns around. "Fine," he says. "Fine. Take your break, Mr. Goodspeed."

It does not get any better the rest of the day. He hardly speaks to me and I do not know how to tell him I am sorry his mother died. The way he is acting, I am wondering if it is even true. All I know is that I have never been so glad to hear the voice say, "Shoppers, the store will be closing in fifteen minutes."

When the doors do close, I am ready to hightail it out of there, but Mr. Kellerman surprises me.

"May I walk with you a ways, Mr. Goodspeed?" he asks. "You live in Shadow Glen, I believe. I am on Fairlawn, just two blocks away from you."

I cannot see any way out of this, so I say okay, and figure he must have his reasons. All I hope is that he is not hiding an ax up his sleeve.

As we walk in silence, he finally blurts out, "I want to apologize for my behavior today."

"That's okay," I go.

"No, it is not okay. I have behaved badly toward you since you began working at Awkworth & Ames and today was the worst. I have been under a great deal of stress, but that is no excuse for incivility."

"Honest," I say, "it's okay. I mean, I know . . . well, I'm sorry about your mom. Dying and all."

"Thank you," Mr. Kellerman says. There is something in his voice that is different, like he is opening a door to a room inside himself that no one goes in usually and he is asking me to step inside and take a seat.

"My mom died, too," I tell him.

"I know," he says back, which surprises me at first but then I remember it's a small town and my dad did work at Awkworth & Ames for a while, back in his drinking days.

We are quiet for a few minutes then, except for the sound of our feet hitting the pavement.

"How do you survive it?" he asks at last.

"What?" I say.

"I wonder how I will survive it."

Before I can say anything, not that I know what to say, he starts pouring words out like they've been living in this room just waiting for a visitor. "I guess I was always something of a mama's boy," he says. "She was terribly protective of me, which I resented when I was young, but I can't blame her. How could I, knowing . . . there was another child, a baby named Patrick, before I was born. He died of crib death at four weeks of age. Can you imagine? That's not even a life. When I came along, she hovered over me and fretted about every little sniffle. I have no doubt she checked on me every night to make sure I was still breathing— probably right up until the time I left home for college.

At school—not college, of course, but elementary school and . . . what grade are you in?"

"Seventh," I tell him.

"Ah, yes. Well, all the way through high school really, I was made fun of. Mama's boy, sissy. I came home crying so many afternoons. And she would stroke my hair and tell me not to listen to them. As if I could help listening to them. But she meant well. She always meant well.

"If it hadn't been for my father, I don't know if I would have been able to leave home and go off to college. He pushed me, insisted that I needed a life of my own. He was right, of course, but at the time I thought he just wanted to be rid of me. He was a very distant man, my father. I never really understood him. Amazingly, I did make my own life. I studied business and met a lovely woman who became my wife. Alice was her name."

We come to a corner and wait for a light.

"Do you mind my telling you all this, Bobby? It feels good to talk."

I tell him no and am struck that this is the first time

ever he has called me by my first name. But I am also thinking how weird it is he is telling me all this, him being a grown-up man and all and me just a kid. It makes me think that Pam was right about his not having any friends and that thought makes me sad. I mean, where would I be without the Gang of Five?

"Alice and I lived in Boston," Mr. K goes on. "That is, until Father died. I never thought they had much of a marriage, to be quite frank with you, but my mother was beside herself with grief. She had always been a bit frail and now she just seemed to come apart. Her only sister lives in California. They were never close. So there was no one but . . ."

"You," I put in. The light changes and we start across the street.

"Me," he says. "Yes indeed. Just me. And Alice, of course, but Alice was not happy about the addition of my mother into our lives. No, she was not. And Mother was adamant about not leaving Paintbrush Falls, since she had lived here all her life, so I had no choice but to return, although I assumed it would be just for a short time. But she became sick, needy. I

203

gave up my job in Boston, went to work at Awkworth & Ames, and Alice . . . well, Alice left me, didn't she? My mother became my only companion. Life grew small. And time endless."

We are walking along Fairlawn Avenue now. I wonder which house is his. I am dying to pee, on account of having had a large Coke during my break and not thinking to go to the bathroom since. It is very distracting, having to pee this bad when you are listening to somebody pour out their life's story.

"I have just had a thought," Mr. Kellerman says as he starts digging in his pocket. "It's quite peculiar. You know how a moment ago I said I never understood my father? Well, here's something, Bobby. I have never truly understood *myself*. Isn't that a terrible thing to say? I am forty-five years old and I do not understand why I have made the choices I have. I have always listened to other voices telling me who I am and how I should live. I *believed* those voices telling me I was a sissy and a mama's boy. I believed my father when he told me I should go away and I believed my mother when she said I should come back. I believed Alice when she said I was a coward and not worthy of her love. Over time, the voices became fewer and fewer until there was only my mother's voice and now her voice is gone. Who is there left for me to listen to?"

He pulls keys out of his pocket as we stop in front of a dark gray house.

"Yourself," I say, and he looks at me like I've spouted something in a foreign language.

I think maybe I have. I think maybe I am spouting a foreign language all the time these days, except that it is really my own language and I am just learning to speak it.

"Mr. Kellerman," I say. "May I use your bathroom? I've got to pee really, really bad."

Mr. Kellerman laughs. Not *at* me. Just because he is surprised, I think.

Inside, after I've peed, I am walking down the hall from the bathroom to the living room and the walls are covered with all these photographs. What amazes me is this: Mr. Kellerman was a kid once. There's a picture of him standing with his parents where he appears to be around my age. He looks happy.

Suddenly, a light goes on and Mr. K is there, nodding at the picture I'm looking at.

"My thirteenth birthday," he says. "We had just come from Tucker's. Remember Tucker's?"

I say yes, knowing that he's referring to the horse farm that burned down a long time back.

"You liked to ride?" I ask.

"Oh, heavens, no, I wasn't allowed to ride," he answers. "Too dangerous. But I loved horses. Mother and Father took me there to feed them, pet them. I knew them all well. I was devastated when that fire occurred, but thank heavens all the horses were saved in time."

He looks at me then and says, "How sad for you to have lost your mother so young."

I shrug, not knowing how to respond.

"We have both lost our mothers," he sighs. "And do you know? We have something else in common. Our names."

"Our names?" I say.

"I'm also Robert."

"Honest?" As if he would be lying.

"Honest," he says with a smile.

He reaches out his hand, which spooks me and I jump.

"I just want to shake hands, Bobby," he says, "a gesture that I hope will signify a new beginning. I regret my anger toward you and I thank you for walking home with me and listening."

"That's okay," I say, and I shake his hand.

As I walk the other two blocks home, I get to thinking about all that he has told me and about the two things we have in common. It is not that I hate Mr. Kellerman, not that I even dislike him anymore, but I can't help it. I hope that those two things are all we have in common and all we ever will.

21

I SLEEP in on Saturday morning, seeing as how I do not have to start working Saturdays until November. Sleeping in is one of my favorite things to do in the whole world. I have a stack of books and comics sitting by my bed and after I wake up, somewhere around ten or eleven, I just reach out my hand and grab whichever one I touch first, and lie there reading until my stomach starts growling. Then I ask, "Are you hungry in there?" and if I get a growl back, I go get some breakfast.

My dad is usually long gone by the time all this happens, on account of his always working Saturdays at the nursery, except in the wintertime.

Well, this Saturday my hand is in the air, not yet making contact with my pile of books and comics, when I hear the phone ring and before you know it my dad is standing there, going, "It's for you, lazybones. Someone named Addie."

I think, *Being a father is like being a stand-up comic in an empty room.* I decide when I am a dad I will not even *try* being funny with my kids.

"Tell her I'll call her back," I say.

My dad hands me the portable phone and goes, "I would, but I'm already late for work. Oh, and there's another reason. What is it again? Oh, yeah, I'm not your servant. I'll see you at dinner."

"Why are you calling me at the crack of dawn?" I say into the phone.

"It's nine o'clock," Addie says.

"Exactly."

She goes into a ramble about how we have to get together to work on her campaign speech, because the assembly is on Thursday and we need time to consider every golden word. I remind her that it is the crack of dawn on Saturday and that is a long way from Thursday and golden words are not like ducks we're going out to shoot and we have to get there early so we can hide before they can see us. This analogy breaks down about halfway so that we spend the next five minutes with Addie going, "What? I don't get it," and me trying to explain it and realizing that it doesn't really make sense, the conclusion of which is my saying, "Maybe you don't want my help writing this speech since I cannot even have a coherent phone conversation."

But Addie is not buying this and will not get off the phone until I promise to come over there around lunchtime.

This I do not mind because both Addie's parents are good cooks and they always have interesting things to eat there, even if they are vegetarian. Besides, I am thinking vegetarian might be a good thing for me to consider becoming since I would not mind parting company with some of my fat cells. I decide to ponder this seriously while making some waffles for breakfast.

Addie's and my attempts at speechwriting do not go well. After a lunch of lentil burgers and vegetable shakes, which are pretty good (except I do not recommend drinking the vegetable shakes in clear glasses since in appearance the word "sewage" comes to mind), we get down to work and Addie hauls out about five hundred index cards on which she has written notes, mostly to do with historical documents. I tell her that I do not think a history of the Pledge of Allegiance or an analysis of the First Amendment is going to win many votes. She gets all huffy about all the time she has put in and all the notes she has taken, and when I tell her maybe she should have put more thought into what she was going to do before doing it, she says, "I take umbrage at that remark."

Umbrage. I swear.

I try to persuade her to take a simple approach, to talk about name-calling and stick to that, but she says this is a *presidential* campaign speech, as if CNN is going to be there to cover it and the middle-school band will be blatting out "Hail to the Chief."

Finally, we give up trying and I say, "What's bugging you today?"

She gets all fired up and goes, "Fine! *I* want to talk about the speech and all *you* want to talk about is stupid Colin and how he doesn't *know* we're going together! Fine! We'll just talk about *that* then!"

"Okay," I say. I wonder: Are all girls like this?

"Fine!" Addie says for the third time, landing on her sofa and scattering two cats. "I just don't understand boys, okay?" I laugh at this. "That's what I mean. *Why* are you laughing? Colin is so dense! I asked him if he would walk me home yesterday and he said sure, and then when I said something about the dance, he was, like, huh? I mean, isn't it *obvious* we're going to the dance together?"

"Obvious to you, maybe."

"Why isn't it obvious to *him?* I hate love."

I know what she means. I remind her about the heart I found in art class, and how it couldn't be Kelsey who drew it but there aren't other girls in class I wish it were from.

All of a sudden, Addie gets all sympathetic, like she's ten years older than me and engaged or something and I'm her pimply little brother. "It's hard to love somebody when they don't love you back," she says, her voice getting all gooey like the marshmallows she doesn't eat because they're made with gelatin and she's that kind of vegetarian. "I'm lucky at least to know that Colin likes me. Even if he is as dense as a . . ."

She stops, not knowing what he is as dense as. I cannot help her out, because my mind is on Kelsey and then I get to thinking about Pam and females in general and my stomach hurts and I tell Addie we should try working on her speech another time, I've got to go.

She says okay, because she recognizes a lost cause when she sees one.

I figure on going right home, but Joe is out on his porch next door and calls over to me I should come in, Pam is about to streak both their hair and do I want to be streaked, too? I tell him no, but I'll watch.

So now I'm in Joe's kitchen and Pam is standing there with Joe's head in the sink and this bottle of coloring that is red. Not normal hair-color red, red like a maraschino cherry.

They're really into it, laughing and teasing each other, and I am looking at Pam and thinking once again how she is the most beautiful creature I have ever seen and that if we were back in olden times she might have been made into a goddess because she is so beautiful. Sometimes I cannot stop my mind. It's scary.

So while I'm having all these thoughts, she says, "Joe told me about the No-Name Party and I think it is so great. I remember what middle school was like for me. It totally sucked. Everybody labeled everybody else. It was *so* easy to hate yourself!"

"Weren't you popular?" I ask, thinking this is like asking the Pope isn't he religious.

Pam lets out a rip-snorter of a laugh then and I think she is going to fall off her stool. "No way!" she gives at last.

"But you're so beautiful," I say. I can't help it, the words just come out. I don't think my having a crush on her is a big secret anyway. She is too smart and I am as easy to read as a Frog and Toad story.

But she doesn't say any of that or make me feel stupid. Instead, she looks at me like I've just handed her every flower in the garden.

"Thank you, Bobby," she says. "But you know something? Being beautiful didn't matter. In some ways, it made things worse. People *expect* things of you when you're beautiful. They expect you to be happy all the time, as if being beautiful is the same thing as being happy. What's even worse is they expect you to make *them* happy. I remember walking into a room one time and everybody broke into smiles, as if I was this surprise package that had just arrived to brighten everybody's day. Maybe it should have made me feel good, but it didn't. I hated it. I felt like I had to be the person they imagined me to be. The fact was I was awkward and incredibly shy."

"You?" I say.

Pam nods. "Kind of like your friend, what's her name."

Joe goes, "Kelsey."

"Mm. I can relate to her. I'm telling you, if I hadn't had my art . . . well, my art saved me, that's all. I ended up going to an arts high school, where I found other people like me. For the first time ever, I felt comfortable, and it didn't matter whether I was beautiful or not."

"You were lucky," Joe points out. "I wish I could go to a school like that. No such thing in this dinky little town."

Pam goes to the refrigerator and takes out juice for all of us. "You're going to have to leave Paintbrush

Falls to find others who are like you, Joe. But meanwhile you've got your friends—hey, thank goodness for the Gang of Five, I wish I'd had what you guys have—and you've got your parents, who are two of the best people in the whole world, and you've got yourself. One thing about you, Joe, you take good care of yourself. You just seem to know how to do that. You have more strength than just about anybody I know."

Joe takes a box of juice from Pam and says, "I wish you didn't have to go back to New York."

I feel a twist in my gut. "Are you moving?" I ask.

"Not right away," Pam says, "but probably after Christmas. A friend of mine called about a possible job opening in a new gallery in Chelsea. Whether it happens or not, it got me thinking about what I'm doing here and the answer was simple: healing. Well, I think I'm healed. Finally. It's time to go back to the city and my life."

"I'm going to miss you," I say, speaking in that foreign language again, the one that I'm learning is my own.

"You are so sweet," Pam goes. "I mean it. I'm going to miss you, too, Bobby. Anyway, I'll be back to visit. Promise."

"You'd better," says Joe.

I finish my juice and tell them I've got to go.

"Why?" Joe asks. "You got something better to do than watch us streak our hair?"

"Hard as it is to believe," I tell him.

As soon as I go home I pick up the phone and dial. I only hang up twice when I hear somebody pick up. The third time, I manage to get the words out. "Hi, Kelsey, this is Bobby Goodspeed."

22

Me: Hi, Kelsey. This is Bobby Goodspeed.

Kelsey: Bobby. Hi.

Me: Um, in case you were wondering if that was me before—

Kelsey: If what was you before?

Me: Those hang-ups. Um, there's something wrong with our phone.

Kelsey: Oh. Did you call before?

Me: Well, yes, but . . . there's something wrong with our phone.

Kelsey: That's okay.

(Long pause.)

Kelsey: How are you?

Me: Oh, I'm fine. How are you?

Kelsey: I'm fine.

Me: I called because . . .

(Long pause.)

Kelsey: Are you there?

Me: Uh-huh. There's something wrong with our phone. Sorry.

Kelsey: That's okay. You were saying—

Me: I was saying—

Kelsey: Why you called.

Me: Oh, because of art. Class. Art class. You know the project we have to do?

Kelsey: Uh-huh.

Me: That we have to decide by Monday.

Kelsey: Uh-huh.

Me: Well, have you decided? I mean, I'm asking you because you're so good in art and I thought maybe you could help me decide . . . Not that I want you to make the decision for me, but I'm having trouble figuring out what I want to do and I just thought . . .

(Long pause.)

Me: Are you there?

Kelsey: Uh-huh. I was just thinking.

Me: Oh, okay. I thought maybe it was my phone

again. Did I tell you we're having trouble with our phone?

Kelsey: Uh-huh.

Me: Do you ever have trouble with your phone?

Kelsey: What?

Me: Never mind.

Kelsey: Okay.

Me: So about the art project.

Kelsey: Oh, right. Well, I'm not sure exactly. It has to be a self-portrait, right?

Me: Right.

Kelsey: So I was thinking of maybe doing a sort of Andy Warhol thing. Do you know Andy Warhol's work? From the sixties? His pop-art portraits?

Me: Oh, sure. Sort of. From the sixties.

Kelsey: Well, I was thinking of doing something like his Marilyn series. It would be easy with computer technology, you know. But I'm not sure. I love Chuck Close's work, too, and I was thinking it would be fun—though really ambitious—to try and do this huge portrait with all the little squares the way he does. Anyway, you could pick an artist you like and model your self-portrait on their work. It would be funny to paint yourself like the *Mona Lisa*, don't you think? Or I heard Justin is going to do a sculpture of himself like *The Thinker*—you know, the Rodin statue? I hope he's planning on wearing clothes. I'm kidding.

Me: That's funny. Planning on wearing clothes. You're funny.

Kelsey: I don't usually talk so much. I don't think I'm helping you.

Me: Oh, you are! Lots! Really! Oh, there's my dad . . . What, Dad? Oh, I have to get off now, Kelsey. Sorry. I—

Kelsey: I didn't hear anything.

Me: You didn't? Well, it's this phone, that's why. We're having trouble with this phone. With all our phones. It's like major phone trouble here. I'm lucky I got through to you. Really. Anyway, I'll see you in school on Monday. Will you be in school on Monday? I mean, you're not sick or anything or going away some-place?

Kelsey: No, I'll be there. Unless I get sick or some-thing or go away someplace.

(Short pause.)

Kelsey: That's another joke.

Me: Oh, right. Good one. Well, I better go. My dad is calling, so . . .

Kelsey: So good luck with your art project.

Me: Thanks. Thanks for calling.

Kelsey: You called me.

Me: That's right. That's what I meant. Thanks, ME, for calling!

Kelsey: You're funny, too.

(Long pause.)

Kelsey: Are you still there?

Me: We've got to get this phone fixed. Well, anyway, I'm glad, thanks for . . . I guess I've got to go now.

Kelsey: Me, too. I'm glad you called, Bobby.

Me: Really?

Kelsey: Uh-huh.

Me: Well, okay. Good. Then I'll see you Monday, okay?

Kelsey: Okay. See you Monday. Bye.

Me: Bye.

23

OF COURSE, there is nothing wrong with our phone.

And my dad isn't even home.

And I have already decided on my art project.

And I made a total fool of myself with Kelsey.

But none of this matters.

All that matters is she said, "I'm glad you called, Bobby."

I can't help thinking, *She likes me.* And even when this other thought comes into my head, the one that says, *No, she doesn't, she likes Joe,* I just push it away and bask in the light of her saying, "I'm glad you called, Bobby."

Monday rolls around and I actually think about what I am going to wear to school, because I do not wish to appear to be a *shlub,* which Joe tells me means "bumpkin" and when I ask him why he doesn't just say bumpkin, he tells me because nobody knows what a bumpkin is. Like they know *shlub*. Anyway, whenever he sees me with my shirt hanging over my pants—this being a favored style of chunky people everywhere—he goes, "Bobby, you look like a *shlub*." For Kelsey, I do not wish to appear shlublike. I put on the coolest shirt I own and tuck it in.

I am hoping Kelsey will race over to my locker first thing and tell me, "I'm glad you called, Bobby," just so I can hear those words again for real instead of in my head over and over, but she does not, although she does smile at me for more than a nanosecond—closer to two nanoseconds—and she waves. These two small gestures practically cause cardiac arrest, so I am thinking that it is perhaps for the best that she does not race over and say anything. Otherwise, I would be dead and the story would end right now.

Of course, the story does not end right now. You could say the story will not end for a long time—until I *am* dead, in fact—because this is the story of my life, except that the part I am choosing to tell you is just a little piece of it. When you're living through it, though, especially when you are twelve and you think the whole world is changing until you realize it isn't the world, it's you, no piece seems little. It's all so big you think it can kill you. But it doesn't. Which is why the story goes on.

At lunch, Addie keeps switching channels between Colin-does-he-or-doesn't-he-know-we're-going-out-together-and-are-we-or-are-we-not-going-to-the-dance-together and the-election-how-am-I-ever-going-to-get-my-speech-written-Bobby-are-you-listening-you-promised-to-help-me. To make matters worse, I keep tuning out because I am checking out the other end of the cafeteria where Kelsey is sitting with Amy and Evie, who are her only two friends, probably because they are also shy. I wonder what they talk about. If they even talk. Anyway, I keep hoping that I will see her stand up so I can wave to her. Then I worry that if I raise my arm to wave, Roger Elliott, who is sitting at the next table, will notice that I have these huge sweat stains (which I do not know if I even have) and will yell out, "Look at Bobby's pits!" and everybody in the whole cafeteria will get to laughing, and so finally I turn around and forget about the whole thing.

"Well," Addie goes, all huffy, "it's about time you started paying attention."

"Yes, Wendy," I say, to which Skeezie winks at me, and Addie clicks her tongue.

"Well, all I can say is, *quel* relief she likes *you*." I realize Joe is talking to me and he's talking about Kelsey.

"But she still *talks* to you!" I say back. "If she *likes* me and she *talked* to me on the phone on Saturday, why isn't she talking to *me* instead of *you?*"

Skeezie pitches in with, "Same reason Addie used to be DuShawn's main spitball target."

We all look at him, then look away quick because he is, in a manner of speaking, eating.

"Explain," Joe says, looking down at his own burrito.

"Simple," goes the Skeeze. "DuShawn is DuShawn, okay? The only way he knows to get the message across to Addie that he likes her is to nail her with spitballs and slip whoopee cushions under her butt."

"Charming," Addie says. "Whatever happened to sending flowers?"

"And Kelsey being Kelsey, well, if she likes somebody, she isn't going to come right out and say so. She's too shy. If anything, she's going to get even *more* shy around the guy she likes. Ergo, henceforth, and in conclusion: Kelsey likes Bobby, not Joe."

"And DuShawn likes Addie," I say, sidestepping the obvious question, Why is Kelsey putting notes in Joe's locker?

Addie furrows her brow. "What about Colin? Doesn't *he* like me?"

Skeezie gives this some thought. I know this because he stops chewing for a good twenty seconds. At last he says, "Colin is a mystery. On the one hand, he shows up at the flagpole at the appointed hour, hands you compliments, and walks you home—"

"*Twice!*" Addie throws in.

"Point taken," goes the Skeeze, "but on the other hand, he declines your invite to hang out at the Candy Kitchen and goes deaf upon mention of the upcoming dance. Ergo, henceforth, and in conclusion . . ." Skeezie is in rare form. "Love is for the birds, and I'm stayin' single the rest of my life."

"Fine," says Addie, "now can we get our minds back on the assembly on Thursday? I've got to give a speech and—"

Skeezie snaps his fingers. "Here is a definite angle," he goes.

Addie says, "Is this about the assembly and my speech? Because if it isn't—"

"It's about Colin," goes the Skeeze.

"Oh," Addie gives, "that's okay."

Joe and I do a rolling-eyeball exchange.

"Maybe," says Skeezie, "just maybe, the reason Colin's havin' a hard time makin' the old commitment is because of the, y'know, *class* difference."

"You mean because he's popular and I'm not?"

"Bingo."

"Oo," goes Joe. "It's so Tony and Maria."

"*West Side Story*," I say, snapping my fingers. "Great movie."

The other two still look blank.

"Duh," Joe says. "You two never saw *West Side Story*? Tony and Maria. The Sharks and the Jets. Two gangs. Can't mix. Boy from one gang falls in love with girl from other gang."

"Oh, it's the same story as *Romeo and Juliet*," says Addie. "Bad ending. People die. I don't think I like that."

Joe bursts into a song from *West Side Story,* which prompts Roger Elliott to holler, "Shut up, you little . . ."

Joe stops singing, but not before we all notice that Roger stopped first.

We lean our heads into the center of the table. "He didn't say it," I point out. "He didn't call Joe a faggot."

"Or a fairy," says Skeezie.

"Or Tinky Winky," Joe tosses in.

"It's *working,* Bobby!" Addie goes, all excited. "Do you think the No-Name Party can win? I mean, I *want* us to, but I never really thought . . . What do you think? Can we?"

"Maybe," I say. "Maybe."

Something happens in that moment. It's not something spoken, not something we acknowledge in any way, but I know we all feel it. For the first time, we consider the possibility that we just might win. That we, the Gang of Five, could actually be winners.

24

ADDIE AND I agree to get together Tuesday night to write the speech. I am still not sure how I got hauled into this except that of the three of us—Skeezie, Joe, and me—I am the best with words and also Addie probably figures I am the least likely to get flaky on her.

The way it works is that all the candidates sit up on the stage in folding chairs, but it is only the presidential candidates who make speeches. The rest of us get to spend the whole time trying to look serious and remembering not to pick our noses or scratch in unseemly places. And of course it is crucial to visit the john right before the assembly. I do not look forward to this event, as I have told Addie a whole handful of times. She keeps telling me, What do *I* have to worry about, I'm not the one giving the speech, which is about as close to sympathetic as Addie ever manages to get.

Before I head over to Addie's house, having neatly worked a dinner invitation into the deal, I show up at Awkworth & Ames to put in my time. Mr. K is calling me Bobby now, except in front of customers, when he still calls me Mr. Goodspeed, on account of putting on a good show, I figure. He is actually being nice to me, and when I make a mistake ringing up a customer's bill, he does not jump on me or even turn his eyebrows into a V, but waits until the customer is gone and says in this calm voice, "Is something weighing on your mind today, Bobby?"

I ask him what would give him that impression and he replies to the effect that it is not like me to mess up and besides which I have seemed a trifle distracted. I own up to girl trouble, at which he smiles, and then I tell him I have to go over to my friend's house later and help write a speech and I do not know what to write.

He gets out of me the whole story about the No-Name Party and how it came about, and the whole time he is shaking his head, which he switches to nodding when I tell him our party motto, *Sticks and stones may break our bones but names will break our spirit.*

"That is so true," he says. "I believed every name I was called in school and took them with me into the rest of my life. I wonder if I might have been a braver person if I hadn't been called a sissy so many times when I was young."

He stops and gives this some thought, then goes on. "Well, there is no point in blaming others, although I do think names belong more to the people using them than the people on the receiving end. But what can we do? We're all so ready to believe the worst about ourselves, we just accept them without even thinking about what they mean or even if they're true."

The voice says, "Shoppers, the store will be closing in fifteen minutes," and Mr. Kellerman goes, "Sorry I can't help you with your speech, Bobby."

To which I say, "You already have."

When I get to Addie's house, I tell her to shush before she even gets five words out, on account of having to write some stuff down. Addie sits there on her bed staring at me until I tell her to stop it, at which point she starts writing, too. And just as I'm finishing up, her mother is calling from downstairs, "Dinner!"

Later, Addie says to me, "What did you write, Bobby?"

I hand her the pad of paper and she starts reading it, then hands it back and says, "Here, you read it to me."

I go, "Why?"

And she says, "Your handwriting is impossible," which I happen to know is not true. I figure she's got some other reason, but I do not wish to waste time trying to get it out of her, so I just pick up the pad and start to read.

It takes me awhile, seeing as how I have written a lot and sometimes it doesn't make sense so I have to fix it while I'm talking, but Addie does not stop me. She just keeps sitting there, cross-legged on her bed, whilst I go on and on, and in the end, she goes, "That's the speech, Bobby, and you've got to be the one to give it."

233

"Me?" I squeak. "This isn't a speech. It's just notes. And, anyway, you're the one running for president, and the presidential candidate is always the one to speak, and, besides, there is no way I'm getting up in front of the whole school and giving a speech. Repeat: no way. And, anyway, this is just notes."

She waits for me to finish and says, "Look, Bobby, I've been working on my speech for over a week now, okay? You saw what I had last week. A lot of blah-blah-blah about democracy and the Constitution and the Pledge. Even though you thought it was boring, I kept working on it over the weekend and I was all set to convince you tonight that it was brilliant and all you needed to do was help me refine it. But the truth is— and if you tell anybody I said this I will kill you, I swear—my speech is a bunch of words and *your* speech is brilliant. Okay, maybe it needs some work to *become* a speech, but I can help you with it and it *will* be brilliant. Anyway, you have to give it because it's all about you."

"It is?" I go, surprised. I don't even see it. "But the rules—"

"We're the third party. We've already broken rules. Or maybe what we're doing is remaking them. Wait, I have this brilliant idea!"

"Brilliant" is Addie's newest favorite word.

She then tells me her brilliant idea and I have to admit it *is* good. "All you have to do is make a few changes at the beginning of your speech, and it will work brilliantly," she assures me.

I look down at the paper and try to imagine myself saying these words *out loud,* not just to Addie, but to all the kids and all the teachers at Paintbrush Falls Middle School. I break into a sweat and my stomach starts to hurt.

"We'll all be there," Addie says, seeing my hesitation. "Skeezie and Joe and me, we'll be up there with you and we'll be part of it. But the words, Bobby, they've *got* to come from you."

"Do you really think I can do it?"

"Absolutely. You'll be brilliant."

I look at Addie and see that she is being serious. "Okay," I tell her. "Okay."

She smiles and says, "Great, let's get to work."

25

HERE ARE some of the things that could have happened on Wednesday and I would not have noticed:

* The school could have burned down.
* Ms. Wyman could have smiled a real smile.
* The school could have been buried in a mud slide.
* Skeezie could have used a napkin.
* The school could have been overtaken by giant fly-
  ing ants.
* Kelsey could have told me she likes me.

Well, okay, I would have noticed that last one, but
you know how it is when you have to do something
really scary, like go to the dentist to have all your teeth
painfully and slowly extracted one by one (which of
course is never going to happen, but you always think

there's the outside chance it *might*) or, as in my case, get up in front of the entire school and give a speech. Not just a speech, mind you, but a speech that when translated into basic middle-schoolese, boils down to: "Ready, aim, laugh!"

If you know what I am talking about, then you will know that it is impossible to think about anything else until you are on the other side of whatever your particular brand of doom is.

From the time I leave Addie's house Tuesday night until eleven in the A.M. on Thursday, all that occupies my mind is the mess I have gotten myself into by agreeing to give this speech. Fine, the No-Name Party is my idea, along with just about everything that goes with it, but does that mean I have to submit myself to ridicule and, worse, the loss of my one true love? Not that Kelsey knows yet that she is my one true love, but after I speak, she will undoubtedly shudder at the mere thought that it might ever have happened.

When I get home Tuesday night, I tell my dad what transpired at Addie's house, expecting him to say, "I'm not letting you get caught up in any left-wing, radical, nutcase politics. I'm calling Addie's parents right now and putting a stop to this nonsense!" But he does not say this. He says, "Good for you, Skip." And, hold on to your seat belts: "I'm taking off work Thursday morning so I can come hear you."

I go, "But, *Daaad*."

He goes, "And I've been thinking about it and I *will* chaperon that dance Friday night, son. Who should I call?"

Wonderful. My father will now be on hand to witness my two greatest moments of humiliation in a life that has been just building up to them.

You may wonder why I think the dance will also be humiliating. Picture this: I will be trying to get Kelsey to dance with me, but she will only want to dance with Joe. Joe will want to dance with Colin, which is not going to happen for a multitude of reasons, including the fact that Colin will be dancing with Addie, unless Skeezie's theory is right, in which case, Addie will be dancing with nobody. So Kelsey will ask Joe to dance and he will say yes, on account of Joe being a dancing fool.

238

So there I will be standing on the sidelines with my shirt tucked in and a Styrofoam cup of punch in my hand, with Skeezie on one side of me, muttering how stupid all of this is and why don't they play some good music (meaning Elvis) and Addie, maybe, on the other side of me, slumping because she doesn't feel good about herself.

And now on top of everything else, my dad will be there, handing out cookies and coming over every fifteen minutes to say, "Come on, Skip, ask somebody to dance. Why don't you and Addie get out there and show them how to do it, what do you say?"

What I say is: Help!

Of course, what I say to my dad when he tells me all this on Tuesday night is, "Great, Dad!" because, do not forget, I was the one who asked him to chaperon in the first place and, as far as the speech goes, I cannot even remember the last time I gave him a reason to want to come to school and see me do anything. So how can I say no?

So that is Tuesday night. As for Wednesday:

One big blur.

(Proof that Kelsey does *not* come up and tell me she likes me.)

Thursday morning I wake before my alarm goes off. I feel sick. I reach for my speech, which I have read over so many times I know I can do it by heart, but I read it over again anyway and I think for the one-thousandth time, *I am going to get up and say these words in front of the whole . . .* and that is when I groan so loud my dad comes in and asks what's wrong and I tell him I am dying.

He does not tell me he will call an ambulance or a funeral director, but instead asks me what I want for breakfast. I tell him Pepto-Bismol.

I carefully select my wardrobe. I finally choose a white polo shirt (tucked in) and khaki pants. I check myself out in the mirror. I am somewhere between preppy and invisible. A good choice.

My dad is smart enough to know that I need to go easy on breakfast. I eat a bowl of cereal and a banana. Every bite sticks in my throat.

While my dad finishes packing my lunch, I say, all nonchalant as if I haven't practiced saying it twenty-five times already, "You know, Dad, if it's busy at work today, you really don't have to come. I won't feel bad, honest. It's not such a big deal."

"If it's not such a big deal," he says back, holding up a fruit leather and a PowerBar for me to choose between and, seeing as I can't, tossing them both in my lunch bag, "then how come most of your clothes are all over your bed? Nice try, Skip, but I'm going to be there. I don't want to make you more nervous than you already are, but—"

"But you *are,*" I go, right away regretting the words.

"I know that," he says. "I was in seventh grade once, too, believe it or not, and I had a father. So I know how you feel. But here's the thing. Your granddad cheered the loudest of anybody at my Little League games—and he came to every single one—and I just about died, okay? At the time, I would have given anything for him to just shut up. I even asked him to stop coming. Which he told me to forget about, by the way. It took becoming a father myself to finally get it. You can't help wanting to cheer your children on, kiddo. That's what being a dad is about. So. I will be there today and I will be cheering for you. Silently. I will not embarrass you, and that's a promise. But I will be there. Now, here's your lunch and there's the door."

I take my lunch bag from him. "It's not you embarrassing me I'm worried about," I tell him. "It's me embarrassing you."

"Ah."

"Did you ever feel that way with Granddad?"

"Every single Little League game. That was the *real* reason I didn't want him there. But I'll tell you what he told me: You *can't* embarrass me. Not ever. It's just not part of the deal."

"Honest?" I say, actually daring to look at him when I ask this.

"Honest," he says. "Now get out of here, or we'll both be late."

Walking to school, I am feeling better, like I just may be able to pull this thing off. Then the doors open and the halls are full of kids hollering at each other and Mrs. DePaolo is walking by hugging her sweater to her shoulders and one of the No-Name posters picks that moment to come loose from its masking tape and fall right on top of Brittney Hobson's head and she looks surprised and then, seeing what it is, laughs her high-pitched cheerleader laugh, like, *I can't believe I let this silly thing scare me!* and I want to turn around and go to the dentist and have all my teeth extracted. Because even *that* would be better than what I have to do this morning.

Addie does not help matters. She is like a cross between the chief executive officer of the world's largest corporation and the chief executive officer of the world's second largest corporation. She is so take-charge I want to tell her to just do the whole thing herself, but then I think, *This is just how Addie gets.*

As for my morning classes:

One big blur.

At ten-thirty, Mr. Kiley's voice says over the loud-speaker, "Will the candidates for the student council please report to the auditorium?"

For the next half hour, I joke nervously with my fellow candidates about fear of collapsing folding chairs and throwing up. I think, *This is democracy in action.*

*I am actually talking to Colin and Drew Geller, and even
Brittney Hobson* (who of course does not admit to any
fears and probably doesn't have any) *and all these
other kids who most times wouldn't even give me the
time of day.* I notice that Colin and Joe are talking and
laughing together when all of a sudden Ms. Wyman
claps her hands and says, "Please take your assigned
seats and let's have a quick run-through. You will not
actually give your speeches now, but we want to be
sure that everyone is clear about the order and how
things will go."

Addie leans past Joe to hiss at me, "Act like I'm the
one giving the speech. I don't want any last-minute
hitches."

"But that's not honest," I whisper back.

Joe says, "This is politics."

To which Addie says, "It's not about politics. It's
about Ms. Wyman. If we let her know we're challeng-
ing one of her precious rules—"

"Ms. Carle," Ms. Wyman goes in a threatening
voice.

"Okay, okay," I say. And we snap back to attention.

The run-through goes quickly and as it happens we don't even get to the No-Name Party, which is presenting last, because classes are starting to file into the auditorium and Ms. Wyman brings the proceedings to a halt, wishing us luck. She goes to each party in turn to do this, and when she gets to us, we are all surprised that she seems so sincere.

"We have our differences, Ms. Carle," she says to Addie, "but I admire your spirit."

Addie's jaw drops about to her knees, but she thinks fast and says, "Thank you, Ms. Wyman."

And then we are left to sit there, and wait, and pray that nothing unnatural occurs.

Because of the lights I cannot tell if my father is out there, but I am pretty sure he is. It's funny, but all of a sudden I wish I could see him.

Ms. Wyman is making her opening speech now, parts of which have to do with democracy in action and the electoral process and parts of which have to do with, "If this behavior doesn't stop right now, we will just cancel this morning's assembly and there will be no elections." When this gets no results, she adds,

"And no dance." And the place gets as quiet as I'm guessing it does in her dreams.

The Democrats go first and then the Republicans. I do not hear a word that Drew or Brittney says. I do hear laughter and applause and cheers, which are loud for Drew and louder for Brittney.

Suddenly, it is our turn and I think I have never had to pee so bad in my entire life.

Ms. Wyman is saying, "This year we have a third party from which to choose. The No-Name Party is a grassroots organization that sprang up in response to a single issue. The candidates are Addie Carle for president, Joe Bunch for vice president, Bobby Good-speed for treasurer, and Schuyler Tookis for secretary. I will now turn the microphone over to the candidate for president, Addie Carle."

I try to ignore the difference in decibel level between the applause that has greeted the previous candidates and that which greets Addie. There isn't time to think about such things, anyway. It is time to put our plan into action. Reaching down under our seats, we each take out a poster board rectangle, which we hold to our chests as we stand up. Each rectangle has our name on it:

ADDIE
JOE
BOBBY
SKEEZIE

We stand there in silence for a moment, then Addie steps up to the mike.

"I am Addie Carle. As you know, I am running for president of the student council on the No-Name Party ticket. Traditionally, it is the presidential candidate who speaks on behalf of the party. But we are a non-traditional party and so it is another of our candidates who will be speaking to you this morning. Our candidate for treasurer: Bobby Goodspeed."

She steps back. There is a smattering of applause. Out of the corner of my eye I see the surprised faces of Ms. Wyman and the others onstage. Colin smiles at me in an encouraging way and I take a step toward the microphone.

Knees, don't fail me now, I think. Still holding my name card, I step up before the microphone. I wait until the applause quiets down and then, without even thinking I'm going to do it, I say, "I'm nervous. I think I need to take a yoga breath." Everybody cracks up at this, Ms. Wyman most of all, and I enjoy the laughter as I take my yoga breath (most of the audience joins in because Ms. Wyman starts out her math classes this way, too, so we're all trained) and then, without needing to look at my notes at all, I begin to speak.

26

These are our names.

Bobby.

Addie.

Joe.

Skeezie.

These are our names. But they are only names. They don't tell you who we are. We have other names, too. Names we have been called, names we have been given. We figured it out. Between us, we have a total of seventy-two names, other than the names you see here. These are names we have been called since kindergarten. The ones we remember, anyway.

Sticks and stones may break my bones, but names will never hurt me.

Anybody who believes that has never been called a name.

This is what I think about names. I think that names are a very small way of looking at a person. When I was in third grade, I got the name Fluff because I ate peanut butter and Marshmallow Fluff sandwiches every day for lunch and also, I guess, because I started putting on weight. But nobody knew why I was eating those sandwiches. I didn't even know myself until this year, when I figured it out. It was because my dad made one for me for lunch one day and he told me, "These were your mom's favorite kind of sandwich." My mom had died the summer before and I missed her. And so from then on I wouldn't eat anything but peanut butter and Marshmallow Fluff sandwiches for lunch. But every time I did, somebody was bound to call out, "Hey, Fluff!" and that hurt.

Another thing I think about names is that they <u>do</u> hurt. They hurt because we believe them. We think they are telling us something true about ourselves, something other people can see even if we don't.

Lardo fluff fatso faggot fairy dweeb mutant freak ree-tard loser greaser know-it-all beanpole geek dork . . .

Is that me? we think. Is that who I am?

If you haven't been called any of those names, think about the ones you <u>have</u> been called. Is that who you are?

The No-Name Party wants to put an end to name-calling in school. We want to start with a No-Name Day, in which we all think about the names we call each other and stop using them—just for a day. Maybe we'll think about more than names and stop talking to each other like some of us are less than others of us. But, hey, I don't want to get too ambitious here. Let's just start with names. No name-calling. For one day. Then we can see where it goes.

Of course, the No-Name Party will do more than this. We want to represent everybody in the school and will work hard to make all voices heard on the student council. We will work with the teachers and the administration to see that the issues affecting all of us in middle school are dealt with fairly and honestly.

So please vote for the No-Name Party.

Wait, there's one more thing I want to say. I didn't plan on saying it, it's just . . . I'm just thinking this as I'm standing up here and . . .

The No-Name Party got started because my friend Addie really believes in the idea of liberty and justice for all. She stands up for what she believes in and doesn't care what other people think. She started the Freedom Party and, well, I won't go into what happened there, but . . .

What I want to say is that Addie has been my friend my whole life, and Skeezie and Joe, for a long time . . . and, well, I think they are the bravest people I know. They are strong enough to be who they are, no matter what names they get called. Even if we don't win this election, I think they are winners . . . I <u>know</u> they are and . . . well, that's all I have to say.

27

I GO to return to my seat. The back of my shirt is so soaked it's on me like a second skin. I see Addie and Joe smiling up at me, and the Skeeze gives me a thumbs-up, and I am thinking, *I did it, it's over.* I'm so relieved, I don't even hear the clapping and cheering at first. It's Ms. Wyman's hand on my shoulder and her voice in my ear saying, "Well done, Bobby," that wakes me up to the fact that the place is going nuts. I turn back and what I see are all these kids I go to school with—a lot of whom have called me the names I've just been talking about—slapping their hands together and cheering, making *woo-woo* noises and circling their fists in the air like I just made the winning touchdown. I think I must be dreaming.

I try to find Kelsey out there and my dad, but I

can't see either of them. I do spot DuShawn at one point, whistling with his two fingers in his mouth, and next to him is Tondayala Cherise DuPré, not showing much of anything on her face but putting her two hands together with some powerful kind of belief.

There is a lot I want to tell you at this point. How everybody all of a sudden jumps up out of their seats going, "Bob-by, Bob-by, Bob-by!" How the next day we win the election by a landslide. How nobody ever gets called a stinkin' name again. And how anybody who loves anybody gets loved back.

But if I told you those things I'd be lying. "Happy ever after" only works out in stories, not in life— leastwise, not happy the way you think it should be. For my money, this story *does* have a happy-ever- after ending, but it isn't the kind that's got anybody chanting, "Bob-by, Bob-by, Bob-by!"

What happens is this:

After a minute or so, Mr. Kiley steps out onto the stage and gets everybody quieted down. He congrat- ulates all the candidates on our excellent speeches and wishes us all luck. Then he tells everybody to proceed in a civilized fashion to our next period class.

Life goes on.

Onstage, we are all talking at the same time, congratulating each other, and while I am still trying to figure out what I should be saying to everybody else, they are all telling me that I gave the best speech ever. And they act like they mean it. Even Brittney. Colin says pretty much the same thing everybody else does, but then he comes back and tells me, "Thank you," like I have given him some kind of gift, which later on I will figure out I have.

As Colin turns away to talk to Addie, I see Kelsey coming up the steps to the stage. I think maybe she is looking to talk to Joe, but she has got her eyes trained right on me and she keeps them on me until she is standing a foot in front of my face and words start tumbling out of her so fast I think she might tip over.

"I will tell you later what a great speech that was," she goes, "but before I lose my nerve and go back to being my shy old self I have to ask you something will you go to the dance with me?"

I cannot believe my ears, but I am feeling brave, too, so I go, "Sure. And, Kelsey, I like you a lot."

To which, she goes, "I like you a lot, too."

Is this a happy-ever-after ending or what?

It is probably a good thing that Ms. Wyman breaks everything up then with, "Come along, everyone, you don't want to be late for your next class," because I don't know what either Kelsey or I would have said to each other next. I am already worried about what we will find to say to each other at the dance, but I do not care. I am beginning to trust that I can find the words when it matters.

I and my friends start to head to class when it hits me that I haven't seen my dad. I am thinking he believed me when I let him think I didn't want him to come. Even after his big talk about my grandfather and all, maybe he decided to take me at my word. I start feeling a whole mix of things—sad, angry, disappointed—when all of a sudden I spot him at the back of the auditorium, leaning against the railing behind the last row of seats.

"I'll catch up with you guys," I say, cutting Addie off midstream. She is totally wired.

"Okay," she says, then tells me for about the dozenth time, "You were brilliant, Bobby."

"Ditto," says the Skeeze.

"Thanks," I go.

That's when I notice Joe isn't with us, but I don't give it a whole lot of thought because I've got my mind on my dad and besides which Kelsey is now giving me a little wave with her fingers and there's a Fourth of July sparkler going off inside of me.

I return the wave and head over to where my dad is.

"Hey," I say.

"Hey," he says back, kind of quiet and respectful, like he's in church. "I didn't come up because I'm having a little trouble keeping it together," he tells me, "and I promised I wouldn't embarrass you."

I do not know what to say to this, but it doesn't matter. My dad is not looking for any more words from me right now.

"You did good," he tells me. "Real good. I'm proud of you. And your mother would be, too."

"Thanks," I say.

We stand there for a minute and then he says, "Skip." And I say, "Hammer." And we hug each other, right there at the back of the Paintbrush Falls Middle School auditorium where anybody could look right in and see us, and I do not even care if they do.

It isn't easy getting through the rest of the day. I mean, who really cares about dividing decimals or contrasting the parts of plants, animals, and one-celled organisms when you've had the kind of morning I have? Not only have I given a speech the whole school is talking about, but I have declared my love for the girl of my dreams. Okay, I may be getting carried away here. I have declared my like for the girl in my art class.

And, by the way, it was Kelsey who wrote my initials in a heart.

All afternoon, everyone is complaining that we have to wait until tomorrow for the elections and there is even a petition going around for next year, saying that speeches and elections should take place the same day because nobody can stand the suspense. Meanwhile, kids keep coming up to me all day wishing me luck. Some even say they're sorry for calling me names; some promise they'll never call anybody a name again. I am thinking that there is no way we are not going to win this thing. Addie and Joe and Skeezie are thinking the same.

That night, we all meet up after dinner at Addie's house to celebrate our victory with ice cream.

The next day, we lose the election.

28

DREW WINS.

But remember what I said in the last chapter about happy endings?

It isn't always about winning the election . . . or the race . . . or the game. Sometimes it is about winning something much bigger.

Here is the rest of the story:

We come in second—a *close* second.

During last period, Mr. Kiley asks Addie and Joe and Skeezie and me—right out loud over the P.A.—if we could come to his office after school. When we get there, he congratulates us on a good campaign and our near victory. Then he tells us that my idea for No-Name Day is more important than who gets elected to student council and will we work with him to help make it happen. We say *sure, of course, you bet,* and he says *thanks.*

And then, just as we're about to leave, he puts a hand on my shoulder, looks me square in the eye, and, I swear on a stack of pancakes, says to me, "Bobby, up until yesterday morning I accepted kids calling each other names. I didn't like it, I put a stop to it whenever I heard it, but for the most part I just shrugged it off as kids being kids. Well, I was wrong. It doesn't have to happen. That was a brave thing you did yesterday, and I want you to know that bravery doesn't go unrewarded. I'm making a personal commitment to seeing that things are different here at P.F.M.S. And that's because of you."

I do not know what to say. I have to bite my tongue from telling him that I like his tie—which I do—because I want to say something nice and am too embarrassed to say the simple thing, which would be *thank you.* He seems to understand this, without my saying a thing. I guess he has been around a few twelve-year-olds in his time.

So the No-Name Party does not win the election,

but No-Name Day, which the following year will become No-Name Week, becomes part of the way things are done at Paintbrush Falls Middle School.

Oh, and about those notes in Joe's locker. They weren't from Kelsey, after all. They were from Colin.

After my speech, Colin got up the nerve to tell Addie and Joe that he needed to talk to them—separately. He told Addie that there was some sort of misunderstanding, that he had thought the notes in his locker were from someone else and that was who he was expecting to meet at the flagpole. He had just figured it was a coincidence she had come by when she did. He told her he liked her, but "not like that," and said he hoped they could be friends. Addie said she understood, and then she was miserable for about five minutes until DuShawn came up to her and said, "Congratulations."

Addie: Thanks. But we haven't won yet. The elections are tomorrow.

DuShawn: I don't mean that. I mean congratulations on your campaign. It's awesome. And Bobby's speech was totally cool. Did you write it?

Addie: No. Well, I helped a little, but mostly it was Bobby's. DuShawn?

DuShawn: Yeah?

Addie: Why did you agree to run for president?

DuShawn: Girl, you are a funny kind of color-blind. You see the color of my skin but you don't see anything else about me. You wanted me to run for president because I'm black. And don't go telling me that's not true, I'm not that stupid. So why'd I agree? I will tell you since you are too blind to see it. I did it because you're smart and you don't take sass from nobody. And I like that.

Addie: Tonni's smart and doesn't take sass.

DuShawn: Tonni's all flash with nothin' behind it. You got more goin' on for you than attitude. Least, that's what I thought.

Addie: You're right, DuShawn. I'm sorry.

DuShawn: Apology accepted. Now, tell you what I'm gonna do. I'm gonna give you a once-in-a-lifetime opportunity to prove to me that you are not color-blind like I say.

Addie: Okay, whatever you—

DuShawn: So you want to go to the dance with me tomorrow night?

Addie: What? You want to take me to the dance?

DuShawn: You deaf, too? I said "go with," not "take." Nobody takes nobody to the dance. But maybe you think I'm not good enough for you.

Addie: No! I don't think that at all! And I would love to go to the dance with you. Really.

DuShawn: Okay, then.

Addie: Okay.

So DuShawn and Addie are going to the dance together and, as it will turn out, they will end up going out together the rest of seventh grade.

As for Colin and Joe, well, Joe does not report his dialogue word-for-word the way Addie does, so I cannot tell you what happened there exactly, but the gist of it is this:

Colin met up with Joe after school on Thursday. It took awhile, but he finally got up the nerve to tell Joe the same things he'd told Addie, in addition to admitting that he was the one who had put the notes in Joe's locker because he thought the notes in *his* locker were from Joe. When Joe showed up at the flagpole with Addie and me that time, Colin hadn't dared come over and say anything. And when Addie had gone over to him, he didn't know what else to do but walk her home.

And then he told Joe that he liked him, and could they go out together.

"Just like that?" I ask when Joe tells me this on Friday. His face is beaming so bright it could bring moths.

"Just like that," Joe goes. "He came right out and said it. He told me he's liked me since last year, but it took him until this year to figure out what it meant, and now he wants us to be, you know, like boyfriends or something."

"That is so cool," I say, and I mean it.

Addie can hardly believe it when she hears the news. "*My* boyfriend is *your* boyfriend?!" she goes, but when we remind her Colin was never her boy-friend and now she has a real one of her own, she relaxes and says, "Maybe we can double-date some-time."

So there will be a whole lot of us going to the dance together, misfits and fits, couples and not. My dad will be there as a chaperon. I'm kind of hoping there will be some single mom there for him to meet. But if there isn't, that's okay, too. The important thing is that he will be there. The way I look at it, love does not necessarily make for a happy ending any more than winning does. What makes for a happy ending is what Addie said all along: freedom. The freedom to be who you are without anybody calling you names.

29

Addie: Today's topic is "What I Want to Be When I
            Grow Up."

Skeezie: That is so lame. What are we, in first
            grade?

Addie: Well, I just thought it would be fun to talk
            about the future.

Joe: I'm going to be famous.

Skeezie: Doing what, if you don't mind my asking.

Joe: Who knows? Something glamorous. It <u>has</u> to
            be glamorous. Maybe I'll be an actor or a
            singer or, oo, I might be a famous designer.

Bobby: What's your name going to be?

Joe: Okay, I've been thinking about that. I have
            two. Ready to vote?

Skeezie: Do we have to put our heads down on our
            desks?

Joe: Wait, was that someone laughing in the next
            booth?

Skeezie: You've used that one already.

Joe: Okay, so here goes: Jade or Soleil?

Skeezie: Where did you come up with those, perfume
            ads?

Addie: What does Colin think?

Joe: Colin thinks I should be happy with Joe.

Bobby: He's right.

Joe: I am sorry, but Joe Bunch is the most boring
            name in the entire universe. Why didn't my
            parents just give me a numeral?

Skeezie: Good one.

Addie: DuShawn says he thinks you're funny, Joe.

Joe: Funny as in . . . ?

Addie: Funny as in funny.

Bobby: Is it bad we're keeping the Forum just for us?

Joe: Colin said he doesn't mind. Besides, we all
            sit together at lunch. Did you ever think
            we'd be sitting at a table with other people?

Skeezie: It's okay, but if Tonni opens her big yap one
            more time about the way I eat . . .

Addie: That happens to be the one thing Tonni and
            I agree on. Really, Skeezie, you could stand
            improvement.

Skeezie: Okay, Wendy.

Joe: She's right.

Bobby: She's right.

Skeezie: Okay, <u>Wendies</u>. I'll tell you this: My future
            does not have a Wendy in it, that's for sure.
            I'm going my own way. When I get old
            enough, I'm getting myself a Harley and I
            am heading out to see the country, man.

Addie: How are you going to make money?

Skeezie: I'll find a way. I'm resourceful. What about
            you, you going to end up being the first
            woman president?

Addie: Maybe. I do think about politics as a career,
            but I don't entirely trust the system. Maybe
            I'll be a lobbyist.

Bobby: You guys are lucky. You know what you
            want to do. I always thought I would stay
            right here in Paintbrush Falls and just
            have a job the way my dad does. Sales or

something. Now I'm not so sure. Ever since
I gave that speech, I'm thinking about
writing. But what would I write?

Addie: You've got lots of time to figure that out.

Joe: You could write about <u>us</u>.

Skeezie: Oh, yeah, we're interesting, all right.

Joe: Speak for yourself. I think we're <u>fascinating</u>.

Addie: And unique.

Joe: And <u>fabulous</u>.

Addie: And amazing.

Skeezie: And different.

Joe: And proud of it!

Bobby: Maybe I will write about us, who knows?
"The misfits."

Skeezie: Uh-uh, man, that's just another name.

Bobby: You're right. We should stop thinking of
ourselves that way.

Addie: We'll just be us.

Joe: "The Gang of Five." That's okay, right?

Skeezie: Totally.

Bobby: Friends forever.

Addie: See, it is fun talking about the future.

Skeezie: Here's something I <u>don't</u> see in our future: food! Geez, the service in this place . . . oh, wait, never mind, here she comes.

Hellomy
nameis
Steffi: How are you doing there, Elvis?

Skeezie: I'm good, HellomynameisSteffi, how you doing?

Hellomy
nameis
Steffi: Aw, you don't have to call me by my full name. You can just call me Hello.

Skeezie: Okay, Hello. You can call me Skeezie.

Hellomy
nameis
Steffi: For real? That's your name? I'll call you Elvis.

Skeezie: Just as long as you call me.

Hellomy
nameis
Steffi: You're one tall drink of trouble, you know that? But you sure are cute. What say you call <u>me</u>?

Skeezie: Really? When?

Hellomy
nameis
Steffi: Five or six years from now.

Skeezie:	Maybe I will.
Hellomy nameis Steffi:	Yeah, and maybe I'll sprout wings and fly.
Addie:	She's funny.
Skeezie:	Ha, ha.
Bobby:	And you're blushing.
Skeezie:	Shut <u>up</u>!
Bobby:	So, Addie, since we're talking about the future, I want to make a toast.
Skeezie:	Can't stop making speeches, huh, Bobby?
Joe:	What're you going to toast, Bobby, fabulous <u>us</u>?
Skeezie:	He's toasting the future, Jade du Soleil.
Bobby:	I'm toasting both. To the Gang of Five: May we all sprout wings and fly.

30

IF YOU are the sort who wonders what becomes of the characters in a story after it's over, I will clue you in to the future.

Joe will end up living in New York City and he will be a famous writer. Mostly what he will write about is his own life, including what it was like growing up gay in the little town of Paintbrush Falls, New York. The name he will be known by is Joe Bunch.

Skeezie will wait five or six years and give Hello-mynameisSteffi a call. They will end up getting married and having five kids. Together, they will buy the Candy Kitchen and bring back the jukebox. The place will become known far and wide for its great food and fast service. He'll call her Steffi; she will never call him anything but Elvis.

It will take Addie awhile to figure out what she

wants to do. After getting three college degrees and spending some time traveling, she will end up teaching social studies in middle school. She will get her students all worked up over questions of right and wrong. Her teaching methods will be a bit unusual, which will result in her getting canned from the first school where she teaches, but she'll stay at the next school until she retires and she will be named Teacher of the Year a record seven times. Many students will be influenced by her. Some will even go into politics.

I guess I am the first one Addie influences this way, because I will go into politics, too. Years from now, people like Kevin Hennessey and Brittney Hobson will open their yearbooks and say, "You know who that is? That's Senator Robert Goodspeed. I went to school with him."

But that's all a long way in the future. Right now, Addie and Joe and Skeezie and me, we've got to make it through seventh grade. And you know something? We will. I swear on a stack of pancakes.

On the Tenth Anniversary of the Publication of The Misfits

The Misfits is dedicated to my daughter, Zoey. It couldn't have been dedicated to anyone else, since it was Zoey's experiences in middle school that inspired me to write the book. I've shared her story with students in every middle school I have visited since the book was published ten years ago, and with many parents and teachers as well. When I asked Zoey once how she felt about my telling her story to so many strangers, she said, "If hearing about what I went through in middle school helps make things better for even one person, then I feel good about it. I'm proud to have inspired *The Misfits*."

I'd like to think that Zoey's story and *The Misfits* have made things better for *more* than one person, but I can speak with certainty only about the one person I *know* has been changed for the better. That person is me. I don't think I would ever have called myself "a get-along kind of guy," as Bobby describes himself before he turns into "somebody who makes a difference," but I can call myself something I never was before: an activist. Thanks to Zoey—and Bobby and Addie and Skeezie and Joe—I regularly find myself speaking in schools and at conferences to young people, parents, and educators, speaking up for what I believe, speaking out against name-calling, bullying, and homophobia.

When I set out to write the book, I had no idea that this it where it would lead. An unfinished short story I rescued from a drawer gave me the characters of Skeezie and Bobby (who had a different name that I've since forgotten); the little town of Paintbrush Falls, New York; Awkworth & Ames Department Store, where a twelve-year-old boy was working, for reasons unknown (even to me), as a tie salesman; and, across the street, the Candy Kitchen and its "back booth with the torn red leatherette upholstery." There, the "gang" waited. But who the gang was, or what they were waiting for, I didn't know. I took that unfinished story and let it lead me where it would—to Addie and Joe and the Forum and Kevin Hennessey and Ms. Wyman and Aunt Pam and Addie's refusal to say the Pledge of Allegiance. I remember writing that scene—when Addie refuses to say the Pledge—as the moment I knew that the novel would go in a political direction, and it would be Addie who would be the driving force.

I'm often asked what elements of the story are real. So:

- Paintbrush Falls, New York: not real, but based in part on the town of Webster, New York, where I grew up. Webster is near Rochester, in the western part of the state. For some reason (possibly to do with my moving from Webster in the seventh grade), I mentally picked up the town and relocated it to the northeastern part of the state, near Saratoga Springs and Albany.
- The Candy Kitchen: real. Not only did the Candy Kitchen in Webster have booths and burgers and ice cream, it sold handmade chocolates (hence its name). As a lover of chocolate, do I have to tell you that the Candy Kitchen was one of my favorite places?
- Awkworth & Ames: real, except for the name. There was a little department store across the street from the Candy Kitchen in Webster, but I don't remember what it was called. Awkworth & Ames just came to me as I wrote.
- Skeezie Tookis: Skeezie's name also came as I wrote, as names often do for me. He is not based

on anyone real, however. A character who is real
is Aunt Pam, who is modeled on my niece Pam.
- Joe Bunch: Joe is *partially* based on someone real.
I'll get to that in a minute.

The Misfits was a surprisingly easy book for me to write.
Once I had my four main characters and the basic situation,
I just let them go where they wanted to and enjoyed the ride.
This isn't to say that I didn't think and plan and plot. I did, but
with greater ease than I've known in writing most of my other
books. I loved the characters from the get-go. They quickly
came to feel like old friends; it was almost as if *I* was the fifth
member of the Gang of Five. So spending time with friends
was one reason the writing went so smoothly. The other was
that I cared deeply about the subject matter of the book. And
I cared especially about the character of Joe.

When I'm asked which character I am most like, I usually
say, because it's true, that I have a bit of each of them in me.
But the greater truth is that I was most like Joe when I was
growing up, although I lacked his self-confidence and wasn't
as "out there" as he is. But I acted "more like a girl than a boy
much of the time," as Bobby says of Joe. And like Joe, I am gay.
I was gay when I was twelve, too, but I didn't have the words to
understand it or feel good about it back then. The only words
I knew were bad ones, bad in the sense of telling me that *I*
was bad. As I have Mr. Kellerman say, "I believed every name
I was called in school and took them with me into the rest of
my life." It took many years for me to realize that the names I
had been called when I was growing up had everything to do
with others and nothing to do with me. When I finally came
to feel good about who I am, I was angry that I had wasted
so much time believing the lies that others (much like the
fictional Kevin Hennessey) had insisted were true. I decided to

rewrite my own story, so to speak, by creating a character who is growing up gay and feels good about who he is, who is the person I might have been had I grown up in a different time with different role models. Role models like Joe Bunch.

It wasn't until I had almost finished writing the book that it occurred to me that schools might take it upon themselves to establish their own No-Name Day, as the characters in *The Misfits* do. Not only did individual schools in different parts of the country do exactly that within months of the book's publication, but a national organization working to make schools safe for all students contacted me about creating a national No Name-Calling Week, using *The Misfits* as its inspiration. When I was asked if I would be a part of this initiative, I jumped at the opportunity. Along with forty other organizations, GLSEN (the Gay, Lesbian and Straight Education Network) has sponsored No Name-Calling Week since March 2004. NNCW now takes place the last week in January (or whenever individual schools choose to participate), and thousands of schools take part annually.

The Misfits and No Name-Calling Week have occasionally come under attack for being part of the so-called "gay agenda," whatever that's supposed to be. But the number of schools where the book is read as part of the Language Arts curriculum or as an "all-school read" and those participating in NNCW far outnumber the few individuals or communities that find the messages of inclusion and respect somehow threatening.

The real agenda, if there is one, is to make schools a place where everyone can be who he or she is, without having to fear ridicule or attack. The first time I spoke about these issues was at Merrill Middle School in Des Moines, Iowa, during the first No Name-Calling Week in 2004. I spoke across a vast gym floor to six hundred and fifty sixth, seventh, and eighth graders arrayed in bleachers before me. I'll be honest: I was terrified. But when I finished speaking, something happened that had never happened to me before. The students gave me a standing ovation. All day long I met with small groups, and later I received letters, and what I heard over and over was this: "You told us the truth." I'm including some of what I said to those students that day as part of the appendix to this anniversary edition. I hope it will speak truth to you as well.

I have always believed in the power of language. Words can hurt. Words can heal. Words can effect change. (I've even co-led a workshop called just that.) Words have been what I have worked with for more than thirty years now. I've written more than eighty books and more speeches than I can remember. After *The Misfits* I wrote *Totally Joe*, to tell Joe's story, and *Addie on the Inside*, to tell Addie's. One of these days, I'll write Skeezie's story, too, because there's so much about him I don't know. And one of the main reasons I write is to ask questions and figure things out for myself.

Oh, there's one change I made in this anniversary edition of *The Misfits*. It's one word, but that one word changes a lot. When I wrote *Totally Joe*, I had the Democrats win the student council election. In *The Misfits*, the Republicans had won. How I missed such an obvious mistake, I'll never know! It was an eighth-grade boy who pointed out the discrepancy during a school visit some time after *Totally Joe* was published in 2005. Since there is only one word in *The Misfits* about the election results—and much more than that in *Totally Joe*—I decided to use this opportunity to make the two books consistent. So you will find that if you happen to read an earlier edition of the book, the first sentence on page 260 is "Brittney wins." If you turn to the same page of this book—and every copy of the book that will be printed from here on out, you will see that the victory now belongs to Drew.

How easy it is to effect change in fiction. One hit of the

delete button and a quick rewrite and presto! The fate of an individual or an entire community can be reversed or set on a whole new course. It is far from that easy in real life. But I hold fast to my belief that each one of us can effect change in whatever ways are open to us. I am lucky to be a writer, to have opportunities to use my words to reach others. The words I used to write *The Misfits* have changed my life and may have changed others. But if I were not a writer, I hope I would still be aware of how words can make a difference. What I say and how I say it—even one word—can affect how others see themselves and look at the world.

Do books change the world? Maybe. Maybe not.

But one thing is certain: People do.

—James Howe

What Can You Do To End
Name-Calling and Bullying?

START with yourself.

STOP calling names and object when others do. Like any other bad habit, you can stop it if you have the will to do so,

THINK before you speak—and then don't speak.

THINK: Why do you need to call the other person a name?

THINK: What would it feel like to be the other person? Remember that in every encounter we meet only a small part of who someone else is. What we see is just the tip of the iceberg.

THINK: What about the other person makes you uncomfortable—and whose problem is it that you feel uncomfortable?

THINK: What real difference does it make to you who they are or what they do?

THINK: How are they hurting you? If they are hurting you, deal with it appropriately. Get help from adults if you need to. If they are not hurting, you: leave them alone.

THINK: What's so wrong about being different? What's so right about being the same?

REMEMBER: The names you call others say more about you than they do about the people on the receiving end.

REMEMBER: Putting other people down doesn't lift you up. It only makes you a smaller person.

REMEMBER: The names you call others belong to you. Just because you see someone a certain way doesn't mean that's who the other person is.

REMEMBER: Being different only means being yourself—nothing more and nothing less.

TRY to stand up for yourself and others.

TRY to respond to being called a name with a shrug or some other form of "couldn't care less." Saying "whatever" and walking away is the perfect response.

TRY to feel good about who you are, hang out with people who see the good in you and don't need to put you down, and do your best to see the good in others.

But there's only so much you can do on your own.
It's crucial that you:

- Be part of a community that says NO to name-calling and bullying.

- When you have the entire community behind you, speaking up, having the courage to do what you know is right, is a whole lot easier.

- Be aware of the messages you get from the larger community—the culture, the country, the world in which we all live.

- Think about all the TV shows you watch in which characters are sarcastic and nasty to one another—often for the sake of a cheap laugh.

- Think about the messages of commercials that tell you how you're supposed to be thin and beautiful and straight and white and blond and sexy and hard-bodied and cool and rich enough to afford whatever products they're selling you—and how much better you're told you're going to feel about yourself when you are all these things.

The messages are everywhere, defining in very narrow terms who we are supposed to be.

Be aware. Be educated. Be kind. Take action.

IMAGINE what a school would be like without name-calling, bullying, meanness, and excluding others.

IMAGINE, and make it happen on your own and as a member of a community working together.